STORIEBOOK CHARM

A SPELLBOUND NOVEL

MELISSA BOURBON

LAKE HOUSE PRESS

Storiebook Charm Copyright © 2020 by Melissa Bourbon Ramirez. All rights reserved. No part of this book may be reproduced in any form or by any electronic or mechanical means, including information storage and retrieval systems, without written permission from the author, except for use in articles and reviews.

Cover design by Dar Albert, Wicked Smart Designs

Published by Lake House Press

This is a work of fiction. Names, characters, places, and incidents are either the product fate author's imagination or are used fictionally, and any resemblance to actual persons living or dead, business establishments, events, or locales is entirely coincidental.

ISBN: 978-0-9978661-4-8

ASIN: B0855TVYY1

The author acknowledges the copyrighted or trademarked status and trademark owners of the following wordmarks mentioned in this work of fiction: Ropers, Texas Rangers, iPod, "Tomorrow," by Chris Young, "Pretty Good at Drinkin' Beer" by Billy Currington, Ariel and Belle (Disney), Jeep, Technicolor, *The Secret Garden,* Red Vines, "Country Girl" by Luke Bryan, Glinda/Dorothy, Prince Charming, Harry Potter, Bibbidi-Bobbidi-Boo

```
Lake House Press
North Carolina
www.melissabourbon.com
```

*Formerly published as Deceiving the Witch Next Door

ALSO BY MELISSA BOURBON

Book Magic Mysteries

Murder in Devil's Cove

Murder at Sea Captain's Inn

Legends Romantic Suspense

Silent Obsession

Silent Echoes

Paranormal Romance

Storiebook Charm, Spellbound book one

Bread Shop Mysteries (written as Winnie Archer)

Kneaded to Death

Crust No One

The Walking Bread

Flour in the Attic

Dough or Die

Magical Dressmaking Mysteries

Pleating for Mercy

A Fitting End

Deadly Patterns

A Custom-Fit Crime

A Killing Notion

A Seamless Murder

PRAISE FOR STORIEBOOK CHARM

Praise for Legends Novels

"An interesting premise and characters that are sympathetic and genuine are at the crux of this romance." ~*RT Book Reviews*

"I felt myself instantly drawn in and I sped through this book in record pace. I couldn't stop reading, as I constantly had to know what happened next; to say that the suspense in this book hit the right notes is an understatement! The La Llorona legend was woven into this story seamlessly and made for a thrilling backstory. And the romance between Ray and Johanna progressed nicely…an excellent read…" ~*Fresh Fiction*

"This book just totally blew me away and I already want to re-read it. [Melissa] is now one of my favourite authors. I must read all of her other books. If you love books with action, romance and a hot heart-stopping hero this is

definitely the book for you. It was completely
phenomenal…" ~*K Books*

"A nice amount of tension in both the suspense and romance plots and this kept me turning the pages.
I particularly enjoyed seeing Vic try to interact with his teenage son." ~*Scorching Book Reviews*

"…lots of action, some romance (but not too much) and characters that you might even feel a connection with on some level. If you like romantic suspense then I think you will enjoy this book… We give it 4 1/2 paws up." ~*Storeybook Reviews*

*Previously published as Sacrifice of Passion and Curse of Passion

Praise for Storiebook Charm

TOP PICK *"Love, laughter, magic, romance, and treachery, this novel has it all."* ~ **Night Owl Reviews**

"…a fast-paced, clever, witty, romantic story with excellent character development and a great plot. I fell in love with Storie, Harper, Reid, and Harper's daughters almost from the first word. The descriptions of Texas were spot on; I could feel the humidity beading on my skin. Ms. Ramirez has an excellent turn of word. I highly recommend this book and anything else she writes!" ~*Fresh Fiction*

"…a nice plot, full of romance and spiced with mystery, magic and fun. I recommend this book to those who enjoy a light, sweet summer read." ~*Bibliophile Mysteries 4 1/2 Stars*

*Previously published as Deceiving the Witch Next Door

Praise for Bread Shop Mysteries

"Wheels within wheels power a dark-inflected cozy." ~*Kirkus Reviews*

"This book has the charm, the characters and the mystery that cozy fans want to read. I am very excited to see where the next book will takes us, and the growth in these characters. This is a must read cozy book for 2017." ~*Bibliophile's Mysteries*

"With the help of her friends, Ivy cleverly cracks open a complex case involving a criminal conspiracy. I loved the emotional nuances of *Flour in the Attic*, right up to the complicated culpability levels of our villains. The cliffhanger at the end also leaves you wanting more, even as the astounding food descriptions sharpen the appetite for all the delicious dishes described within." ~*Criminal Element*

"The complicated relationships between Marisol's adult children, their father, and their step-father ensure that the plot is compelling while the mystery increasingly complex. Few will see the horrific twist that motivates an all-too-possible crime, but they can rest assured that Ivy and her friends will see justice through and continue deliver comfort through their extraordinary bread and ethnic cuisine." ~Kings River Life

"Mouthwatering food, a quaint setting, vivid characters, and a stunning mystery. The first person voice is engaging and perfectly styled, and there is a nice blend of humor and heart." ~*Reading is My Superpower*

Praise for Magical Dressmaking Mysteries

"This series debut by Bourbon…has a clever premise, lots of interesting trade secrets, snappy dialog, and the requisite quirky and lovable family…A fun read…" ~ _Library Journal_

"A charming, whimsical tale that's also chock full of sex, lies, intrigue, and murder…one heckuva series debut. Harlow is a marvelous heroine. Smart, funny, and full of fire. Bourbon's supporting cast is remarkable, as well – a perfect blend of quirk, menace, and heart…the image-conscious, richer-than-God Kincaid family could have been plucked straight from an episode of Dallas; and hunky architect-slash-handyman Will Flores and his young daughter Gracie add heat and warmth (respectively) to the story." ~_Night Owl Reviews_ TOP PICK

"This is a fun read, perfect for vacation or, if you're like me, holed up on your bed turning the pages at 2 AM to find out what happens. I'm looking forward to the next installment in this new series." ~ _Stitches and Seams_

"How can you not like a character that can drink a hot cup of Joe as easily on a sweltering day as she can on a chilly 40-degree one and calls herself a "Project Runway," "Dancing with the Stars" and "Iron Chef" kinda gal." ~ _AnnArbor.com_

"Pleating for mercy is an engaging novel! It kept me up late, wanting to know how all the details worked out in the end, and making sure my favorite characters were as friendly as I had imagined. I loved how fabric was woven into each part of the story, as the characters weave their own tale." ~ _Amy's Creative Side_

"This is the first book in a blissfully enchanting and

entertaining series that I hope is here to stay." ~ _Notes from Me_

"Harlow is a clever, down-to-earth main character who you can't help but like. Most of the action takes place right in her dress shop, and Harlow asks all the right questions as she tries to figure out the murder mystery….Fans of cozy mysteries will want to be sure to put this one at the top of their "to be read" list." ~ _Two Lips Reviews_

"What can I say about this debut series? "Charm"(ing), intriguing, and satisfying; a page-turner with the right touch of potential romance and paranormal just about covers it." ~ _Once Upon a Romance_

Praise for the Lola Cruz Mysteries

"Fans looking for the next Stephanie Plum might just find her in Sacramento in the form of Lola Cruz, the muy caliente heroine of Misa Ramirez' Living the Vida Lola…Ramirez puts together a snappy blend of mystery, romance and humor…" ~ _Mystery Lovers Book Store_

"Ramirez keeps the action tight, the plot smart and humor light in this spicy blend of crime solving and romance. Lola's Latina perspective adds extra sizzle." ~ _Publishers Weekly_

"This highly entertaining first-person novel launches a new series with a bang. Well written with laugh-out-loud humor and a complex mystery, this wonderful debut will have you looking forward to more books in the series. Lola is no lightweight detective, despite the chick lit feel to the book, and the balance between her personal and professional life is ideal. The tension in both romance and danger deepens expertly." ~ *Romantic Times Magazine, 4 Star Review*

"A true chick mystery: Hot, seductive, flirtatious, sexy with some true PI work on the side." ~*Book Lovers Bookstore*

"I love the characters in this book from Lola, Jack, Antonio, Reilly and her relatives and how they interact with Lola's occupation. This was a fun and sexy read and I can't wait for the next book in this series." ~ *Notes From Me, 4 star review*

*For the real Storie and the Storiebook Café,
both of which inspired this magical tale.*

STORIEBOOK CHARM

PROLOGUE

Eight years ago...

Whiskey Creek, Texas, wasn't far from Austin, but to Reid Malone, it might as well have been light years away. Thank God for the lake. No matter how much he hungered for city life, this place—especially on a day like today—was his solace.

He parked on the bluff in between the trees near the old haunted fishing cabin, popped open a beer, and readied his fishing pole. Maybe it was college life and worrying only about himself that he missed when he was stuck in his hometown. Back here he had his dad and the bar to worry about. He needed to earn a little cash over the summer, but he was already counting the days till he could get back to the city and put his newly minted diploma to use.

Dark clouds pooled in the distance. A storm was coming in, and it made him breathe easier. There was nothing like the vast Texas sky. In the distance, loud rolling thunder cracked and flashes of lightning streaked through it. Before long, the sky would open, the rain would fall, and the temperature would drop twenty degrees in a matter of minutes. Being here helped put things in perspective for him. The big sky and the power of the storm helped him to not take things so seriously and made the long summer months ahead seem manageable.

The thunder cracked again, and that's when he saw her.

Storie Bell.

She tore over the dirt road in her daddy's beat-up old truck, the tires kicking dirt until she skidded to a stop not a hundred yards from him. But she never looked his way. He cast out his line, just watching her. She had to be twenty years old now. What was she was doing here by herself?

It took her a good while to get out of the cab, but when she did, he nearly dropped his pole. He'd seen Storie around town a few times and he knew she was pretty in an offbeat way, but now? In her cutoff jeans and white T-shirt knotted below her breasts—luscious, beautiful breasts, from what he could see—she was all curves and flesh and bronzed skin. Her hair, like no color he'd ever seen, shimmered in the fading afternoon sunlight. The coppery tint was almost otherworldly, he thought, leaning forward in his lawn chair.

He'd heard tales about her strange behavior and quirky habits, but all he could think was that she was a damn siren. A girl next door who could bring a man to his knees with one crook of her finger.

She released the tailgate and climbed into the back of her daddy's truck, standing on the edge, raising her arms like she was trying to harness the thunder that was slowly rolling in. At first he thought she was just trying to capture a breeze and stay cool in the humid July heat, but then the clouds moved faster and turned in the sky in time with her rotating hands. He couldn't tell what she was up to, but a silent alarm sounded in his head. "What the hell?"

He was so enthralled that he finally gave up trying to fish. He tossed what was left of his beer into the garbage and moved into the shadows of the trees. She might need help, he reasoned. What woman came out to the lake in this kind of weather unless something was wrong?

His attention never wavered as he got closer. God, she was beautiful. And now he had the best view he could get out here in the open. He didn't know her, and certainly wouldn't act on his attraction for her, but hell if he didn't want to memorize every last detail of her face and body now that he was seeing it spotlighted as she stood on the tailgate.

She moved like a blade of grass, softly swaying in the fading sunlight. Her arms stretched upward, her head tilted back. She stiffened, just for a split second, and a shudder passed through her. Thunder cracked overhead, a flash of lightning sparked through the dark clouds...was it seconds later?

He stared at the sky. That wasn't right. The order was wrong. Lightning came first. Thunder came from the shock wave from the heat, then cooled off the lightning bolt.

Before he could wonder about it any more, Storie jumped down from the tailgate and plowed headlong into the lake. Somewhere in the distance, a cat wailed, as if sounding the alarm. Shit. Reid jumped up, starting toward the water's edge. "Christ, woman, what are you doing? You don't swim during a lightning storm!"

She kept going, striding forward against the force of the water. He froze, waiting. Watching. She stalked through the muck, finally bringing her arms overhead and diving under the water.

A network of light broke through the clouds, a crash of thunder following. The right order this time. Maybe he'd imagined the reversal.

His breath clogged his throat as he counted to ten in his head, waiting for her to break the surface. Ten came and went. And then fifteen. He searched the dark water. Where the hell was she?

Something had to have really upset her for her to come up to the lake alone with a storm brewing, and what in the damnation had she been trying to do up there on the tailgate? Had she been drinking? Was she trying to get electrocuted? Could she even swim? Oh, Christ, if she were drowning...

Without another thought, he ripped off his shirt as he raced to the water's edge.

He just hoped they both didn't get electrocuted.

He dove under the water, but it was brown and murky and he couldn't see. He swam, breaking the surface to get some air, then ducking down again to keep searching. Above him, the sky flashed with light. The boom of the thunder traveled through the water like a muffled drum.

For a brief moment, the lightning allowed him to see under the water, but there was no sign of her. Panic swarmed his cells until he could hardly think. He was too late.

But then his arm brushed something that recoiled from his touch. Storie!

He kicked off the soft, smooth bottom, pushing himself in the direction he thought she'd gone. He peered in front of him, frantically searching until he made contact again. This time, he shot upward, dragging in a ragged breath and getting his bearings.

The clouds had grown darker, but it was still light enough to see. Bubbles popped where he thought she was. So she'd come up for air. He lunged, but then stopped as her head appeared, breaking through the surface of the water. And then, just as he'd imagined it, she rose like a mermaid, water cascading off her dark hair, off her skin, off the T-shirt clinging to her body.

"You're okay." He exhaled, catching his breath and reorganizing his thoughts.

Wide-eyed, she gasped, turning to him. He wasn't positive, but her eyes looked red-rimmed, as if she'd been crying. She blinked and sank back down so that only her shoulders and head were above water. Her eyebrows knitted together and she dipped her chin, peering at him. "Reid Malone? Is that you?" She didn't wait for an answer before asking, "What in tarnation are you doing? You scared me half to death!"

And just like that, she'd turned the tables, making him feel guilty for trying to help her. "I thought you were drowning."

"I wasn't." She'd reached the part of the lake where she could stand. This time when she rose from the water, she was like a phoenix, all fire and glory against the backdrop of the orange, yellow, and red streaking the horizon. She walked toward her truck, water dripping from her cutoffs, from the white T-shirt still knotted at her rib cage.

"Yeah, I can see that," he said, coming out of the water behind her. He swallowed, stifling every bit of his physical reaction to seeing her. "Next time you're not drowning," he said with a low growl, "I'll just leave you to it."

She stopped at the tailgate, putting one hand on the edge of the beat-up truck, and then, like the damn siren he knew she was, she turned to face him. "You do that, Reid," she said, real slow, her soft Southern accent as luscious as her body. Her gaze flicked to his chest—and below, before rising to his eyes again. "You take yourself a good long look, because this has been a crap day. I'm leaving Whiskey Creek in the morning, and this is the last you'll ever see of me."

He heard what she said. Crap day. Leaving Whiskey Creek. But all he could do was swallow and drink her in. Long legs, curvy hips in those low-rise shorts heavy with water, the corners of the pockets slipping down farther than the edge of the shorts themselves. And that T-shirt, sticking to her body, plastered against her curves.

Oh yeah, he took a good long look—every bit of her seared into his brain, from the light dusting of freckles across her nose to the beauty mark on her stomach.

And everything in between.

CHAPTER 1

Present day...

Storie Bell was a witch. Not the kind that lived in Harry Potter's world. No, she was more like Glinda, the good witch of the North, minus the munchkins and Dorothy.

Only when she tapped her heels together three times, she didn't suddenly fit in. Didn't miraculously have the life she longed for. But things were about to change, no thanks to magic. She and Harper Patterson stood in front of 13 Houston Street, gazing up at their futures.

"You know," Kathy Newcastle, the town's premier—and only—real estate agent, said from beside her as Harper hurried off to meet a delivery truck, "now that you're finally here and moving in, I can tell you. You almost lost this place."

Storie turned to the agent. "How so?" Saying the dilapidated old gas station was a fixer-upper was a colossal understatement, but it had good bones and it was hers, left to her by her father. The idea of anybody else wanting it was just crazy, but to her, it was a treasure in the rough. A place she could make her own and settle into.

"Jiggs Malone did everything he could to make a deal with your daddy. He wanted this place, but bad."

"Why?" Storie shot a wary glance at The Speakeasy, the bar right next to her new business. There wasn't a chance in hell she'd let any Malone have a piece of anything belonging to her. Her father might have claimed to like Jiggs, but she knew better. There was bad blood there. Maybe not as vicious as the Hatfields and McCoys, but enough that she didn't trust a Malone any farther than she could throw him. Well, given that she had her witchcraft and could hurl him halfway across town, she revised her sentiment. She didn't trust a Malone any farther than her best friend, Harper, could throw one.

Kathy looked up and down the street, as if she were readying to reveal a big secret. She'd hit the half-century mark, but her sun-scorched skin, combined with the poofy style of her chestnut hair, aged her another ten years. Kathy, though, hadn't shied away from Storie despite the whispers and murmurs of the townsfolk about Storie having unnatural powers.

"I can't say for certain," Kathy said, "but I do know it has something to do with the bigwigs who've been coming around to the bar for the last six months. Jiggs has some deal cooking. Maybe he thought he could buy the place, fix it up, then flip it real quick. His clock is ticking, if you know what I mean."

Jiggs Malone had seemed ancient back when Storie was a senior in high school. She knew he was probably about sixty-five or so. Plenty of years left. Sounded suspect to her, which meant there was more to the situation than what Kathy knew. Her jaw tightened at the very idea that Jiggs had tried to buy the place from her father. More reason to steer clear of any and all Malones.

A couple came up the sidewalk toward them, slowing as

their gazes met Storie's. They whispered something to each other and kept walking, nodding curtly as they passed. No matter how many years had gone by, it was something Storie would never get used to.

"Don't mind folks," Kathy said, giving her arm a light squeeze. "People talk, but they'll come around."

Storie looked back at her new business. Before long, a sign would be hanging from the *porte cochere* and swinging in the breeze. The Storiebook Café, with the tagline, *Where happy endings begin...*

Mixed and matched pots would overflow with multicolored flowers. And inside? Coffee. Tea. The best food this side of the Brazos River. All with the added bonus of books.

"The Storiebook Café," she said, her voice dreamy and far away. "It'll be a novel experience." She laughed at her own bad pun, but in truth, it was just what she was after. Something fun, quirky, different, and a place to call home. She could have relied on her vision and her magic...but she was determined to fit in this time. No more moving around because she couldn't control her powers. She'd use a spell here and there, but they'd hired a good contractor because that was the only way to appear normal, and Storie was done being an outsider in her own life.

Alone.

Isolated.

Lonely.

But maybe Kathy Newcastle was right. Maybe folks would come around, stop their whispering about her, and just let her settle down in the one town she'd called home, albeit briefly, during her childhood. "I hope so," she said.

"It's about as perfect as it's going to get," Harper said, coming back to join them, her Southern accent as thick as honey dripping from a hive.

"Thanks to the contractor," she said. "Where'd you find that man?"

Kathy waved at a woman across the street. Behind her, a mangy stray dog trotted across the courthouse square, disappearing around the corner of the old limestone building. The woman lifted her hand, stopping for a minute, staring.

Would folks ever be able to just accept her?

A dark cloud suddenly pressed down on Storie and a chill spiraled slowly through her. She got this feeling more and more often, almost as if some darkness was seeping into her bones. If only she could hide her magic, she'd be okay, but she'd learned over the years that hiding her powers didn't really work. Everywhere she'd lived, her magic surfaced in one way or another, and people talked.

"Mr. Garland? I've been in the business long enough to find the best people," Kathy said. "Once everyone sees what you've turned this place into, and if they come to your grand opening, I'm sure they'll love it."

Storie and Harper both gaped at her. "What do you mean *if?*" Harper asked. "Why wouldn't they come?"

Kathy snuck a look at Storie, sighing. "People around here have memories like elephants."

Harper rolled her hand in the air, prompting Kathy to go on. "What does that mean?"

Storie's skin pricked. She knew exactly what Kathy was talking about. More than anything, she wished she could erase the past, but she was stuck with it, like a shadow that followed her everywhere.

Kathy's eyes flashed and suddenly seemed laced with suspicion. "It means rumors about Storie still run rampant around here." She turned to face her. "You only lived here a year, but that's long enough to make an impression."

"What kind of impression?" Harper demanded, her accent barely softening the edge in her voice.

Kathy hesitated before finally turning to Storie. "Let's just say that folks are still a little spooked when they think about the books all flying off the shelves in the high school library, or the water in the lake as hot as a bathtub. Now you and I know you had nothing to do with any of that, but when folks can't explain something, they have to place the blame somewhere—"

Harper scoffed. "And they blame Storie? What, like she's a witch, or something?"

"She happened to be nearby every time, so it's easy to add one and one together."

Harper threw a pointed glance at her before muttering, "Ridiculous," under her breath as she turned and walked away. Harper was Storie's only real friend. They'd met when Storie moved back to Somervell County, first settling in Clement, and then, finally, ready to stop letting her past and her powers dictate her choices, she'd come back to Whiskey Creek. Harper and Harper's two daughters were as close to family as she'd ever get.

"What if folks don't come?" Storie asked, half to herself, but loud enough that Kathy heard.

"They'll come," she said. "This town needs a bookstore, and it needs a coffee shop."

Whiskey Creek had its share of restaurants and even had a bakery, but no coffee shop. Nothing but The Speakeasy right next door, and another dive on the road out of town.

"You're giving them both," she added.

"Where people can find their happy endings," Storie said, but she wondered if she'd made the right decision.

Magic drained Storie, especially magic involving objects outside the natural world. She couldn't explain it, but there it was. She wondered if it had something to do with being around non-witches. Could too much of the ordinary world zap the witchcraft right out of a girl? Was that what had broken up her parents and chased her dad away from the magical realm?

She didn't have the answer to that question, and likely never would. Her thoughts drifted back to the library incident. Justin Davidson had followed her around town for days. Finally, at the library, he'd gathered up enough gumption to ask her to prom. A normal girl would have giggled or flirted or just said yes. But not Storie. No, her nerves made her magic go haywire and the books started flying off the shelves, hurtling to the floor and forming enormous piles. Justin turned white and backed away, they did not go to prom, and the whole incident had put her in bed with a fever for two days.

The scalding lake water had been a test. She just wanted to control her powers. How else was she supposed to practice? But that exercise, while less trying on her body, had still made her tired.

The energy drain was one reason Storie had always been so careful to keep her powers at bay, especially around Harper. Mortals and witchcraft didn't mix. That was the biggest lesson her father had taught her, and one she took to heart. If Harper knew the truth, it could cost her their friendship, and Storie wasn't willing to risk that.

Her calico, Miranda (named after Miranda Lambert, of course), rubbed the side of her body against Storie's leg. Storie crouched, running her hand in long strokes across her back. "I know," she murmured so only the cat could hear. "It's not ridiculous to worry that nobody will come, is it?"

She knew, in fact, that it was completely true. But Whiskey Creek had always felt like a real home, and this time she was going to do whatever it took so it would be different. She was counting on it. All she wanted was to settle down and blend in.

Miranda meowed, as if to tell her that, yes, this time it would indeed be different. And then she scampered off.

"Buddy's doing right by you?" Kathy asked about the contractor.

"So far," Storie said. Harper nodded.

"Your daddy knew Buddy Garland, Storie."

Storie tilted her head. "Did he, now?"

"Sure did. They go way back."

Her dad had never mentioned Buddy, but then again, that wasn't a huge surprise. He'd been horrified that his one daughter was a witch, and he'd done everything in his power to hide from it. Secrets. His life had been full of them, and now that he was gone, she knew there were a whole lot more that she'd never know.

Six months had gone by since he passed, but the veil of sadness still happened unexpectedly. It happened despite the secrets and their differences and even though he'd never understood her. How could he? He was mortal and she wasn't, and he'd never let her forget it. She'd borne it like a curse, hiding who she was from everyone. It wasn't like witches just roamed the streets with people saying, "Hey, have you met the witch next door?"

She missed her dad.

Kathy laid the back of her hand on Storie's forehead. "Bless your heart, sugar, you look chilled to the bone. Everything will work out just as it's supposed to."

Kathy hadn't added the word *hopefully,* but Storie knew she'd thought it.

She waved away the reassurance. "I'm fine." But that darkness had seeped in again, unsettling her to her core.

Thinking about the mother who'd abandoned her always brought those feelings to the surface. She'd erected a thick brick wall around herself after her dad had told her the truth eight years ago. What twenty-year-old woman wanted to learn that her mother had given her up? Storie preferred the fairy-tale version in her head, the one where she was an ordinary girl who'd had a mother and father who loved her, and had a place to call home. The one where her Prince Charming would show up and accept her for who she was, and where she found her happily ever after.

But if her own mother had completely washed her hands of her child, what were the odds that a man, let alone her Prince Charming, would ever show up? And if he did, that he'd accept her for who and what she was?

No, Harper and her daughters were as close to family as she was going to get.

She looked back across the street, but the square was deserted. The woman who'd stopped for a minute was gone now. No surprise, given the heat. Far too hot to be milling around.

Slowly, the darkness faded and she felt like herself again.

She blinked back the tears that had threatened to pool in her eyes. So what if she was destined for a life without a man? And who cared that her mother had given her up so easily? Her daddy had done his best and thanks to him, she and Harper were making a go of The Storiebook Café.

"Harper found a great little house," Kathy said. "Are you sure you don't want me to find you a place, or maybe you're not sure if you're here to stay?"

Storie smiled. Kathy wasn't spooked by the idea that she might be a witch. Making a sale, that was what she was after, and she could put up with the unexplained if it meant a commission.

She shook her head. "I'm not going anywhere, but I'm fine in the loft above the shop."

A movement from behind one of the windows at The Speakeasy caught her eye.

Kathy noticed. "Your daddy spent a lot of time over there," she said. "God rest his soul," she added.

Storie cupped her hands over her eyes and peered at the brick building with the old saloon doors. The place looked like it could have been on a Hollywood lot, straight out of a Western. The women fell into a moment of silence. She hadn't ever realized how lonely her dad had to have been, always on the run. Always trying to protect her. And later, spending so much time alone in a bar. If it hadn't been for her, he might have fallen in love again. Had a different life. She pushed her guilt away. "It's an old building."

"As old as your place. Been in the Malone family for as long as I can remember. 'Course Jiggs is knocking on death's door. Bad ticker. Then again he's been that way for a long time. His little stint in the pokey didn't help. But he's a cantankerous old coot if there ever was one."

"He was in jail?"

Kathy nodded sagely. "Moonshining," she said, her voice low. "But he got off. Some big liquor company's ready to pay a pretty penny to get their hands on his hillbilly pop. Don't know why he doesn't sell. I hear it could be worth millions, and well worth it. The stuff is pure heaven."

Storie didn't care about moonshine, but she was curious about what had happened to Jiggs's son. Just thinking about him still sent her heartbeat racing, setting her on edge when she thought about it. That day at the lake… "Where's Reid these days?"

Kathy's lips rose into a little smile. "He was just in California visiting with his mama. Got back yesterday, if I'm not mistaken."

Storie got the feeling that Kathy was rarely mistaken. "He's here?"

"Sure. He pretty much runs the bar now, although his mama taught him that he was too big for a small town."

She stared at Kathy. Reid was here in Whiskey Creek? She swallowed, trying to get rid of the image of him that was emblazoned in her mind for always. Just thinking of him now sent a wave of embarrassment through her, heating her from the soles of her feet to the crown of her head. She'd barely known him, but the way he'd looked at her that day at the lake, like a wolf stalking his prey... She shivered. "He *runs* The Speakeasy?"

Kathy shrugged, her poofy hair rising and falling with the action. "He keeps to himself. Takes care of the bar and his daddy. Between you and me, I think he wants nothing more than to make tracks on outta here and shake Whiskey Creek's dust off his boots."

Leaving Whiskey Creek was exactly the opposite of what Storie wanted. She was going after her dream, no matter what it took. She didn't understand what would hold a man somewhere he didn't want to be. "Then why does he stick around?"

But Kathy just shrugged again. She looked innocent as she said, "He could handle his mineral and gas rights from anywhere, but my guess is that he's too committed to Jiggs to run out on him. If I were you, I wouldn't get myself involved with him."

Her spine stiffened at the warning. "Not that I would, but why?"

Kathy flashed her million-dollar smile. "Jiggs wanted to buy your building, and I've heard him say he still wants it. Reid wants his daddy happy. I'm just sayin', I wouldn't trust him if I were you. When he wants something, he sets his mind to it and you might find yourself signing on the dotted line if you're not careful."

Storie bristled. There wasn't a chance in hell that she was going to have anything to do with Reid Malone. *Enemy* might be too strong a word, but after that night at the lake...and now, hearing how he and Jiggs had tried to take what was rightfully hers?

"I don't have anything he wants." But she tucked the warning away. "And since he never steps foot outside, I'm not likely to see him, anyway." She scoffed, staring at The Speakeasy, as if he could read her lips. "And he probably doesn't even read," she added, as if that was worst of all.

"'Course he reads." Kathy looked Storie up and down with a scrutiny that made her back go up. Her gaze traveled to the shop behind her for a second before settling back on her face. "And I'm pretty dang sure that he'll want *something* from you."

"And I'm pretty sure he won't," she said, although it gave her a little thrill to think that he might. An image of Reid Malone flashed in her mind. Six feet tall, broad shoulders, rugged. He'd been gorgeous from what she remembered, in an antisocial, dangerous sort of way. Her cheeks heated at the mere idea that he'd want her, and she pushed away the thought. Her dad had made it perfectly clear: she was a witch and couldn't be with a mortal man. It was why she'd run away from Reid in the first place.

A horn blared on the opposite end of the square. Kathy turned to look as she answered. "You can tell yourself that, sugar, but he's gonna be on you like a fly on honey."

Storie ignored Kathy. She might be an expert at real estate, but that didn't make her an expert on Reid Malone... did it? "I'm here to stay, so if he's on his way out of town, then that's that."

Kathy pressed her palm to her chest. "You made the right decision coming back here. I think Whiskey Creek is the perfect place to settle down. Kinda gets under your skin and takes hold, doesn't it? Sure did for your daddy."

Just not for Reid. For Storie, there was just something about this little town. The Courthouse Square. The lake...

This was where she belonged. She felt it in the very depths of her soul. "Why does Reid want to leave Whiskey Creek?"

"I reckon he'd have to answer that one," Kathy said. "This venture you have is gonna be great, especially for Harper and her girls."

Storie put on her game face. "I always say, when life gives you lemons..." She trailed off because she really *could* concentrate, flick her wrist, and turn those lemons into lemonade, but she kept *that* to herself. She'd do everything she could to just fit in. "You're coming to the grand opening?"

"I'll try, but I've got a lot going on, and well..."

Storie finished the sentence in her head. Kathy could sell Harper a house and help with Storie's title transfer, but that didn't make them friends. Before she could say anything more, Kathy handed her the keys, gave her a little wave, and said, "Off to make another deal. Ta *ta!*"

Storie walked toward the door, but stopped when that darkness crept into her again, working its way through her veins as if it were a snake slithering through her body. She looked up and down the street. Empty sidewalks. Awnings and flags billowing in the light breeze, but no people. The sky was clear, not even a single cloud forming above. Nothing. But something wasn't right. It was as if she were being pulled toward some invisible seam that divided this world from some other place. The place where she'd been born.

She steeled her will, rooting her feet to the ground. "Fight it," she muttered under her breath. But how could she fight what she couldn't identify?

Harper had wandered off again a few minutes ago, disappearing around the corner with her daughters, but now their chitter-chatter grew louder, filling the quietness as they came back into view. The girls skipped ahead, stopping to lean over the brick planters, and yanked out a few new weeds as Storie propped her sunglasses on top of her head to hold back her copper curls. She closed her eyes and let her imagination run wild, not difficult to do considering her imagination was the thing that had sustained her on a daily basis.

Only the image that popped into her head wasn't her Prince Charming, and it wasn't even Reid Malone.

It was a faceless woman. Her mother.

Strange.

She looked back at The Speakeasy, starting when she saw another movement. Was that a shadow moving behind the window?

Reid.

She pushed him out of her mind, joining Harper, Scarlett, and Piper with the weeds.

"Add flowers to your list," Harper said.

"Those pretty ones you grew in the pots in Clement," Scarlett said, gazing up at her with a toothless smile.

"Astrids," Piper said.

"Good memory." The little lavender flowers resembled bluebonnets, but they had silver centers and were the one thing her father had brought with him from the magical world. Everything else had left a bitter taste in his mouth after his breakup with Storie's mother. He'd called them astrids and she'd planted them, using her magic to keep them growing year-round.

"I will," she said, ruffling Scarlett's hair.

Today she was seeing her new reality. The gas station had been completely repurposed. Come spring, vines would climb up the boxy brick columns alongside the asphalt drive. She tilted her head and considered the bare columns. They needed the vines now.

If she was really careful not to arouse suspicion, she could get a few flowers to grow before the opening.

Piper's voice interrupted her thoughts. "Will a lot of

people here buy books? 'Cause I don't wanna go back to Clement," she said, a sharpness in the nine-year-old's tone.

Storie looked at Harper's daughters. Together, they'd become the four musketeers. As makeshift a family as there ever was, and Storie would never give it up. "We are making a go of it, and you're not going back to Clement."

But she looked at Piper and Scarlett, who both stood gaping at the building, the stacks of two-by-fours, the table saw, and the last of the appliances to be installed in the kitchen. There wasn't much to be done, but to them, she knew it seemed like an unclimbable mountain. The place hardly looked like a fairy tale, and it didn't seem like the kind of place where people would find their happy endings.

She bent down and wrapped Piper up. "It'll be great," she said. "Just wait."

But the darkness settled over her for the third time, and she knew that it wasn't going to be as easy as she hoped.

She felt someone's eyes on her. Reid, peering from behind the cover of The Speakeasy? Or...

Over Piper's head, she let her gaze drift, let her magic take over to identify who was watching.

The woman she'd seen across the street. She stood in front of the old limestone courthouse, staring at her. Their eyes locked and Storie felt as if she were being pulled by a strand of gossamer, sticky and inescapable. A shiver passed over her. In her mind, as if someone was whispering to her, she heard, *Time to come home*, over and over and over again.

Who was she, and what did she want?

Storie's breathing grew shallow and she closed her eyes for just a moment. When she opened them, the woman was gone.

* * *

STORIEBOOK CHARM

*R*eid Malone leaned against the dark wood molding at the front window of The Speakeasy, admiring the view. Namely Storie Bell. Being able to look at her was the only upside to the entire situation. What the hell was she doing back in Whiskey Creek, anyway? And right next door? Her being here just added a huge complication to his plan, which was to search the old station, make sure his dad's secret stayed just that—a secret—and to find the thing Jiggs needed to make his deal.

He'd never planned on coming back to Whiskey Creek, and he certainly never thought he'd see her again, but thanks to the multimillion-dollar deal on the table from Gemstone Spirits Company for Jiggs's Apple Pie Moonshine, and because of his dad himself, Reid *was* here. They were the two things keeping him in this little town, but Storie...Storie would make things interesting before he left again.

And right now, that meant keeping secrets and searching for the missing ingredient Jiggs needed to finalize negotiations with Gemstone.

She infiltrated his mind now, just as she had years ago, and no matter what he did, he couldn't shake her out of his thoughts. He was two years older than her, and finishing up his sophomore year of college by the time she'd moved here during her senior year, but word traveled in a small town and every time he came home to visit his dad, he'd gotten an earful about the eccentric girl who'd come to town.

She'd carved her way into his head that night at the lake when he'd saved her life, and it had taken every ounce of restraint not to take her right then and there. He'd wanted to, more than he'd wanted anything, and the memory had been emblazoned in his mind ever since.

"What's going on out there?" His father peered through

the flattened wooden slats covering the windows of The Speakeasy.

Reid knocked back his cowboy hat. "Looks like the business next door is going to open soon." And from the smile on Storie's face, she looked happy. Like she was really settling down in Whiskey Creek. Dammit. Everything would have been so much easier if only he'd been able to buy the place from Ted. But Storie's dad had no interest in selling, so now he was going to have to devise some other plan. Hell, he was going to have to get creative, but if it saved his dad's hide and kept Storie out of trouble, so be it.

Jiggs let loose a string of curses that would turn even the toughest cowgirl red in the cheeks. "I want what's mine. This deal with Gemstone has to happen," he said. "We need it, son."

"I know, Pop. Simmer down, would you? You're going to give yourself a heart attack."

He guffawed. "Not like that hasn't happened before."

"Yeah, well, we don't need it to happen again. I'm taking care of things." He just had to be careful, that's all. Besides, it wasn't like he'd helped his dad. He'd only just found out about it when the suits at Gemstone came poking around and Jiggs fessed up. Reid had given him a month to get everything in order before it was all going to be shut down.

Which meant time was running out.

Jiggs shuffled over, his shoulders hunched, his skin weathered from a hard life in the Texas sun. "What kind of plan you got cookin'?"

"The kind that'll get me inside next door so I can look around for real." But with Storie and her friend renovating the old place—which gave him heart palpitations—he wasn't able to get in there and search. The Speakeasy and what was now The Storiebook Café shared an outdoor room. There didn't *seem* to be any access to it from inside the old filling station, thank God. At least none that he'd found so far, but that didn't mean it wasn't there. If Storie discovered what was happening out there, he and Jiggs would have some explaining to do and their deal with Gemstone might go to hell.

Not to mention the guaranteed jail time. He could lose everything, but that garden room was his father's lifeline, and Reid would risk it all to give his dad what he needed.

"You gonna rustle up some ghosts and scare the bejeebers out of 'em?" Jiggs let out a raspy chuckle, but doubled over as it turned into a hacking cough.

Reid laid one hand on his father's back, the other holding him up by the shoulder. "Let it pass, Pop," he said.

"You better get that plan into action right quick, son. The clock's a-tickin', and I won't never find no peace in the hereafter unless you get what's ours so I can leave my legacy on the world."

Reid nodded. His father's days here were numbered. He loved his dad and had come back to help him out and spend some time with him, but once he made the deal happen and Jiggs was settled, it would be time to move on again. He could manage his mineral rights holdings through his lawyer, visit Whiskey Creek on occasion, and everyone would be happy.

When he was here, he longed for the city, and when he was in the city, he longed for the simplicity of small-town life. But no matter what, he knew Whiskey Creek wasn't enough. His mother's words, and her leaving, had made settling down in a place like this too risky an endeavor. What woman would be satisfied with a town the size of a postage stamp, would raise up a family, and would love both the small-town guy and the businessman sides of him? They either wanted one or the other, but not both.

His mother had always told him that she was too big for

such a small town. He'd grown up wondering if he was, too, and if that's where his discontentment stemmed from.

Reid had tried to tell his dad that he had enough money to last a lifetime and back, but it was Reid's money from his mineral and gas holdings, and Jiggs wanted his own. He wanted to leave something behind that had *his* name on it, and who was Reid to deny his father that?

He'd heard the story his whole life. The old moonshining still that old Gus Malone had operated. The secret room with treasure and pieces of history tucked away for safekeeping. Jiggs had spent the last five years researching and investigating every square inch of Whiskey Creek in hopes of finding that elusive room, finally narrowing the location down to someplace in the vicinity of The Speakeasy and what was now The Storiebook Café.

Over the last few months, Reid'd been in and out of the old building next door as much as he'd dared, searching the best he could. Of course it didn't help that he didn't know precisely what he was looking for. A definite flaw in successfully executing his search plan.

Jiggs shuffled back behind the bar, leaning heavily on his cane. Reid watched him for a minute. Giving his dad the one thing that would set him at peace was more important than his desire to get out of Whiskey Creek. What he wanted could wait. He'd give Jiggs his last wish.

He turned back to the window and watched Harper and her two girls pull weeds from the brick planters. His attention shifted as Kathy Newcastle waved good-bye, leaving Storie standing in front of the corner building, staring up at it. He'd been keeping an eye on her during the renovations, waiting for an opportunity to sneak in and have another look around, but someone was always there and the opportunities were getting slimmer and slimmer.

He folded his arms over his chest, never taking his eyes

off her. At twenty-eight, she had just the right combination of experience and rebellion. He could see in her the defiant tilt of her chin, the way she threw back her shoulders, and her hand propped on her hip as if she were ready to give someone a good what-for. Maybe it was her auburn hair and the bright copper highlights, or maybe it was the faded, ripped blue jeans and tank top. Whatever it was, every time he looked at her, he was reminded of the summer after he graduated from college.

Don't think about it. But the memory exploded in him, just like it did on a regular basis. He couldn't stop it.

He'd never really known her, but seeing her that day had ignited a desire in him that had gripped him. He knew enough of her story—growing up all over the place, never settling anywhere. Looking at her now, seeing the old gas station come to life, he was smart enough to know that she needed roots more than anything else, and she wanted them in Whiskey Creek. A place to belong. A home, especially now that her daddy was gone.

Ah shit. He felt like hell for messing with her now, but what else could he do? A fissure of guilt built in him over the fact that he was set to deceive her.

Angrily, he shoved his guilt aside. There was no way in hell he'd let his thoughts go there as he ripped apart the empty beer boxes, tearing them down to little pieces. He stood up for what he believed; that was the bottom line. And right now he believed in helping his father get what he needed before he left this earth.

Reid took one last look at Storie, banishing the temptation that had built in him since that day at the lake, right along with his curiosity about her. He couldn't be distracted. Gemstone Spirits would be back before long, and if the recipe for Apple Pie Moonshine wasn't tested and ready, his dad's deal would go south. And he couldn't let that happen, not when that was the only thing getting his dad up each morning, the only thing that helped him get through each day.

Reid wouldn't let his dad lose that deal, or that accomplishment. He'd do what it took to get into the building next door and find what he was looking for, if it was the last thing he ever did for his dad.

CHAPTER 2

Six o'clock was well past Buddy Garland's normal quitting time, so where was he, and why was the front door open wide? And if he was still here, why wasn't he chattering away to himself, or blaring Billy Currington's "Pretty Good at Drinkin' Beer"? Which Storie suspected might be true for Buddy Garland.

An uneasy feeling gnawed in her gut, the same intuitive gnawing she'd felt just before she discovered her ex, Randy, cement specialist of Clement, Texas, and his secretary, Mary Lou, laying rocky aggregate together six months ago.

Her powers were a blessing and a curse. Sometimes she didn't want to know that something bad was about to happen. Then again, there was something to be said for being prepared.

Miranda, her calico, often appeared at times like this, almost like a prewarning, but she was nowhere to be seen and Storie couldn't put her finger on anything in particular, so she pushed her worries aside.

"Everything'll be just fine," she said quietly, looking at the mess of tools scattered about, the to-do list in her mind growing longer by the second. Harper was at the market stocking up on supplies for the grand opening. She and Harper both had their tasks and knew exactly what still needed to be done.

Piper, who was a solid nine going on forty-five-year-old girl, stared up at Storie, her pudgy arms folded firmly across her chest, drawing her thoughts away from Buddy Garland and Randy Yocum. "It's worse than the old junkyard near Daddy's work," she said in all her little-girl wisdom. "Have you and Mama lost your everlovin' minds?"

"Yeah, Storie." Scarlett, Harper's six-year-old, and Piper's mini-me, stomped her red cowboy-booted foot. "Have you? Have you both lost 'em?"

Storie laughed, putting her sunglasses back on to block out the glare of the still-bright sun before she looked down at the two of them. "Why, because it's not done yet?"

They nodded in unison.

"We'll get everything done," she said, tucking her hair behind her ears, "and here's a little advice. First, if you're gonna stomp your foot, you have to do it right. A double stomp is much more effective." She demonstrated, and Scarlett mimicked, giggling until her dimple appeared in her cheek. "And second of all, your mama's fine, but I most definitely *have* lost my everlovin' mind." She leaned in to whisper. "But between you and me, I kinda like it that way, and you should aspire to it."

Scarlett's eyes grew to the size of saucers. "Really?" she said in an amazed whisper.

"Really. And I know precisely where mine is, so don't you fret."

Scarlett dropped her hands to her side and gazed up at her like she was Alice in Wonderland standing ten feet tall. "Where is it?" she asked. "I won't tell." She trailed one finger in an X across her chest. "Cross my heart."

Storie lowered her glasses to the end of her nose so Scarlett could see her eyes, then she darted her gaze at the gas station. "It's in there," she said. "Safe and sound."

Piper rolled her eyes. "Her mind is not in there, Scarlett," she said with the inflated attitude of an angsty fifteen-year-old.

"Oh yes it is. Come on, I'll show you." Storie dragged them both inside the front door and into what was now the main room of the bookstore/café (and what had been the convenience store), prattling on about the flowers and the swinging sign, but hoping she'd find Buddy Garland along the way. Without her contractor, all her promises would turn into lies.

There was no sign of him.

"Look at the bookshelves," she said, gesturing at the long wall straight ahead. They were stained with a dark walnut finish and were already half-filled with books. "There's going to be a sliding ladder and a window seat, too. Back there"—she pointed to what had been the service center of the gas station—"is the kitchen." She listened for the *tap-tap-tap* of a hammer, or the sound of a drill. Nothing. "Tables and some cozy chairs for reading will go right in the center. They'll be here tomorrow. Your mama and I have been waiting to surprise you—"

"But where's your everlovin' mind?" Scarlett wanted to know.

Storie hid her smile as she reached toward the ceiling, fisted her hand around thin air, and then, with a notch of her finger to make a spark, flattened her palm against the top of her head. "Back, safe and sound."

Scarlett's cornflower blue eyes grew bigger, but just for a moment. She was a wise little girl and couldn't be fooled for long. "That wasn't your mind," she said.

"Gee, really?" Piper shifted her weight onto one leg and

arched an eyebrow up, a talent she inherited straight from Harper. She tucked the book she was reading under her arm.

"Really," Scarlett answered earnestly, not picking up on her sister's sarcasm.

Storie crouched and wrapped her arms around the girls, who were probably the closest things she'd ever have to her own children. "The Storiebook Café. Your mama and I dreamed up this place before either of you were born. It'll be your legacy. It's going to be magical. Just wait, you'll see."

"I can't see it," Piper said.

"Me, neither," Scarlett added, stomping her foot twice.

"Your imaginations are getting sketchy, I'm afraid." Storie wagged her finger at the girls. "We may have to get your mama and play some dress-up to recharge them."

Scarlett stopped stomping and squealed. "Can I be a mermaid? I wanna be Ariel."

"Absolutely," Storie said. "How about you, Piper? Who are you going to be?"

She slid the toe of her very practical brown boot across the sawdust-covered floor. "I guess I'll be Belle."

"You're always Belle," Scarlett said.

"So? I like Belle."

"You just like her because she's the only princess who reads."

"She's not even a princess—"

A rattling sound from the garden room (formerly known as the repair bay) cut Piper off.

"Whoa! What was that?"

"Is there an evil queen back there?" Scarlett whispered, her chin quivering.

"We don't live in a storybook, Scar." Piper's deep frown said she didn't believe in fairy magic anymore. "There's no evil queen."

Storie could argue that point. In her opinion, a mother

who abandoned her daughter was certainly evil, if not precisely a queen. "It's just Buddy," she said. Probably digging through his tools or collapsing his ladder. Thank God. As long as he was working, they'd finish in time for the grand opening.

"Is it a king, then?"

Piper rolled her eyes, but before she could dash her sister's beliefs, Storie said, "Come on, let's go check it out."

As they walked through the tearoom and into the garden room, Storie made mental notes of everything that still needed to be completed between now and the grand opening in a week and a half. From dusting the built-in bookshelf on the far wall of the tearoom to creating some semblance of order in her minuscule office at the far end of the kitchen, there had to be a hundred things, at least. The list felt endless. Or it would, to a non-magical person.

Working her magic at night was an option, but reenergizing after using that much of her powers would drain her. Which meant getting work done during the day would suffer.

Realizing her vision was no small task.

Turning a rundown service station into a magical café that sold a few equally magical books might well fail before it ever really started. But no amount of magic could make people come in and spend their hard-earned cash. She couldn't impose her spells on others against their free will.

There was a lot it could do, but even magic had limits. They'd caught a glimpse of Buddy moving his ladder from one place to another and left him to his work, heading back to the front room.

"When do the people come?" Scarlett asked, looking up at her with her big brown eyes.

That was a good question, and another thing that gnawed at Storie's gut. Aside from Harper, she hadn't ever connected with anyone. So far, folks had stopped by to see what the new business on the corner of the town square was, but they poked their heads in warily, withdrawing again just as quickly, as if they were afraid she'd actually be able to cast some spell and turn them into monkeys or give them coiled pigs' tails.

From the big front window, she saw that mangy dog sitting across the street, staring straight at her. A silvery shiver worked its way up her spine, but it wasn't from the dog, she realized. No. A man strode down the sidewalk, heading her way. He looked familiar, and then, just like that, she placed him.

Reid Malone.

"Good lord," she muttered. She shooed the girls into the back, ducking into the kitchen to have a little time to think and where she could watch his progress.

He looked good. *Really* good. He'd been grown up when she'd seen him last—finished with college—but eight years had aged him in all the right ways. He'd been a good-looking boy, if you were into the bad-boy cowboy thing, and he was an even better-looking man. Strong and settled and confident. The soul patch just under his lower lip was new. Or at least new to her. And damned hot.

When had blue jeans, cowboy boots, a T-shirt, and a cowboy hat become so sexy? She'd never gone for that good ol' boy type, but Reid was like a tall drink of water.

But she thought about the Carrie Underwood song. He's the devil in disguise, she reminded herself. Kathy Newcastle had been abundantly clear about that. He'd do whatever it took to get what he wanted, and she was sure he'd want something from Storie. She remembered all too well how persuasive he could be. That night at the lake, all her senses had left her as he'd closed the distance between them and she'd actually considered succumbing to his charms on her last night in Whiskey Creek. If he wanted her now, it would only be in passing, since he had one foot out of town.

"Not going to happen," she muttered. She was here to stay. Putting down roots. A one-night stand wouldn't fly in her book. "Pass on by." She waved her hands above her head like an air traffic controller. Best to just steer clear of each other.

She tried not to think about the last time they'd seen each other at the lake when she'd been twenty, but her breath hitched as she watched Reid amble toward the café. He had to be thirty now, maybe even thirty-one. He lived in a cowboy state, and while he might not be a rancher, he had that rugged look to him, all hat and swagger.

His last memory of her had to be that same night at the lake. It had taken every last bit of courage for her to do it, but if she was leaving Whiskey Creek, she was leaving on her terms, not all worked up over her mother, or over Reid Malone. She'd mustered up all of her gumption and had slowly turned around to face him, dripping wet.

Her cheeks heated, even now, remembering how she'd taunted him. "You take yourself a good long look, because this has been a crap day. I'm leaving Whiskey Creek in the morning, and this is the last you'll ever see of me."

He'd taken a long, lingering look, and then he'd moved toward her. "Maybe I can help you forget."

"Impossible," she'd said, but she'd looked into his eyes and wondered if, just maybe, he really could help her dull the pain.

Her skin rippled at the memory. When she thought about it, she could still feel the heat of his eyes on her, taking in every inch from the top of her head to the tips of her hot pink toenails.

She acted without even thinking, reaching her hand up, cupping her palm against his face. The next instant, he gripped her hips and sat her on the hood of her daddy's truck, tugging her forward again.

And then he'd dipped his head to her neck, sucking and nipping as her back swayed, the wet cotton of her shirt plastered against her skin...and against his chest.

Slowly, he picked at the knotted fabric, finally undoing the tie and peeling the T-shirt from her damp skin. Then his thumb hitched over the waist of her soaked denim shorts before it broke free, moving down her hip and settling on her thigh.

Lord have mercy. Dull the pain. Her mind lost the ability to think rationally. Instead, she let go, losing herself in the moment. She'd never see this man again. Succumbing to an hour of pleasure and then leaving would be easy.

It felt so naughty. She didn't know Reid, although she'd seen him around town a few times. Never imagined that he'd be touching her like this.

Oh God. Just thinking about it now, and how she'd barely been able to stop herself before the lightning struck and the thunder rolled and the lake water churned. He hadn't noticed any of it, thankfully, but the moment—and what had almost happened between them—had kept her awake nights ever since.

There was something about Reid Malone, mortal or not, that was magnetic. She'd been drawn to him that night, and she was drawn to him now. Thank goodness she'd become smarter over the years. She wore a bra, for one thing, and she had no plans to ever lose control again the way she had that night.

Through the window, she saw him tip his cowboy hat back, just a touch, before letting it settle on his head. There wasn't much breeze today, and the humidity had to be at 80 percent, but he looked fresher than he had a right to be, and she...she was a mess after working all day.

"Keep walking," she muttered again.

No such luck. Being a witch had its drawbacks. He just breezed through the front door like he owned the place, and there wasn't a damn thing she could do to stop him. He had to think she was just a common hussy. After all, what kind of woman would let a man touch her as she had? Her cheeks heated just thinking about how she'd let him kiss her neck and then dipped his head...

Oh God. Her mind fogged.

And if he didn't have sore feelings over how she'd dismissed him so thoroughly that night, he sure would when she rejected him flat. Because if he'd come to finish what they'd started at the lake that night, well, he could rest assured that it wasn't happening.

No matter how charming he tried to be, with that smile, or the faintest dimple on one side, or the swagger he carried, or that damn cowboy hat and the tuft of hair under his lower lip, she knew he was not her friend. Kathy's warning came back to her. "He'll do whatever it takes to get what he wants."

She spied on him as he looked around the front room of the shop and she dragged in a few breaths. He was a hell of a lot more handsome than she remembered. A little bit of his hair peeked out from under his black suede hat. Darker than she remembered. Not quite black, but a deep mahogany that was like a bold cup of Sumatra coffee. His eyes were just as intense, and full of secrets. Deep, fathomless eyes that couldn't be trusted.

She couldn't stay in the kitchen and stare at him all day, no matter how appealing he looked. And how safe she felt with a wall between them. She was a witch, but if he was relentless in his pursuit of things, he just might be able to wear her down. And that would end in heartache.

She raced into the tearoom, deciding whether to go upstairs or not. Harper hurried out of the garden room, her arms loaded down with bags of groceries, one of them torn and haphazardly held together. Storie grabbed the bags and set them on the table, yanking Harper behind the door of the stairwell, batting the bundles of astrids she'd conjured and hung upside down to dry out of the way.

Harper stared at her, wide-eyed. "What's going on?"

"Nothing," she whispered. She thought about muttering a spell under her breath, something along the lines of a giant hook that could drag Reid back outside and far, far away from her. But, number one, she didn't happen to know that spell off the top of her head, and number two, even if she did, using an enchantment on him meant outing herself. A giant hook was sure to be a dead giveaway.

"Hiding in the stairwell isn't nothing. Are Piper and Scarlett—?"

She patted the air. "They're fine. It's Reid Malone," she said quickly. "He's in the front and I—"

Harper grinned. "*The* Reid Malone? The one you told me about? You're afraid to see him?"

Storie made a face. She pressed her ear to the door, listening.

"What are we waiting for?" Harper whispered. "You're not going to be able to avoid him forever, you know. Kathy Newcastle told me he pretty much runs the bar next door."

"I know, but I can avoid him right now." She held her finger to her lips and cracked the door open. She edged forward, Harper on her heels. The heavy clap of Reid's boots against the floor sounded as he ambled through the shop, nosing around as if he were looking for something. He pulled a few books off the shelves. She imagined he glanced at the front, the back, flipping them open to the front page, before sliding them back into place and moving on. It's what people did, after all. A quick perusal that decided if they'd give the book a shot.

"I knew he didn't read," she murmured.

She held her breath, waiting for what seemed an eternity. Finally, she couldn't take it anymore. Her unsummoned magic had stopped her from making a mistake with him once. This time, she was going to use it to get what she wanted. She might not be able to make him turn and leave against his will, but she could force the issue.

He had to have a cell phone. She made sure Harper wasn't looking at her and concentrated on it, picturing it in her mind, and then circled her wrist and whispered a spell that would send Reid a text message.

Something *pinged* and a second later his boots clicked against the floor as he headed for the door. "You can't get rid of me so easily twice. I'll be back, Storiebook," he called into the empty room.

Goose bumps rose on her skin. He wasn't even going to pretend. He wanted something from her, and she feared this was all-out war. The shop? A do-over of the night at the lake? Both?

He might be back, but she wasn't the same torn-up girl she'd been. "Bring it on, Reid." Next time she saw him, she'd be prepared.

CHAPTER 3

THAT NIGHT, after yet another run to the hardware store in the neighboring town, Storie parked her Jeep in front of The Storiebook Café. A chill wound through her. Ten o'clock in the evening, and still a scorching 97 degrees, but she shuddered as if someone had just walked across her grave.

Except, of course, that she wasn't dead and was nowhere near a cemetery, and sensing ghostly spirits was not one of her abilities.

She peered up at the cheese moon, shadowed and pockmarked in the velvety sky. She caught a movement from the corner of her eye and searched the dark shadows of the square. Nothing was there, but another tremor danced over her skin. She shook it off, stuffed her keys in the pocket of her jeans, and headed to the café.

Those barren flowerbeds pulled her up short. This was what she'd come for. She'd promised Scarlett and Piper that she'd plant the astrids, but had to do it when no one was around. The veil of night made her feel safer. Peering over her shoulder, looking this way and that, she made sure no one was out and about on the square. Utterly deserted.

Perfect.

She skirted deeper into the shadows, imprinting in her mind the flowerbeds as she wanted them to be, rather than as they were. She concentrated all of her energy on the image in her head and closed her eyes. Time came to a standstill for her, but she knew it all really happened in a brief moment. The tingling started in her core. She felt a swirling, could see the colors of the rainbow blurring together as they spiraled inside of her. The sensation spread from her solar plexus outward, twining around her nerves and muscles, twisting like a coil of energy until her toes and fingertips burned.

The vision in her head seemed to pop, suddenly more vibrant. Her body shuddered, a release overtaking her. She gave into the sensations coursing through her, letting her body feel every nerve as if each had been singled out, isolated, and magnified.

Her breath grew shallow, her knees weak, but colors splashed in her mind in Technicolor and she knew without seeing that, in a sudden burst, the flowers had sprouted in the planter boxes.

But, as usual, the effort to use magic drained her. She felt weak in the knees, and dizziness swept through her. She drew in a bolstering breath to recharge.

"So the rumors are true."

A male voice jolted her out of the moment, the prickling of her skin going cold, her powers instantly ceasing. A complete letdown. She knew who it was from his fresh-cut-grass scent, as well as from the rugged timbre of his voice and the faint Southern drawl that gave just a hint of gentlemanliness to it. She knew it before she ever turned around.

Reid Malone.

His simple statement sent her heart plummeting to the pit of her stomach. Had he seen her do magic? She'd barely hidden her powers from him at the lake that night, but now, had she blown everything—her future in Whiskey Creek—all for some flowers?

She had no choice but to turn. But she threw her head back and faced him head-on. "What rumors?"

One side of his mouth lifted in a sardonic smile. "Hell freezing over, and all that."

So maybe he hadn't seen. She shook off the last remnants of the magic that flowed through her, sneaking a quick peek at the flowerbeds. The little magical astrids bloomed in profusion. Lavender and white daisies created a whimsical backdrop. It wasn't finished, but it was a start.

She put her hands on her hips, tamping down the bubbling anxiety in her chest and the wave of dizziness washing over her from the spell. Damn it, but Reid's sudden presence made heat rise to her cheeks as if he'd caught her having an orgasm rather than doing magic—not that being discovered doing one was better than being discovered doing the other. "What are you talking about?"

His smirk stayed firmly in place as he said, "I seem to recall you telling me that you were never coming back to Whiskey Creek. You didn't say unless hell freezes over, but it was sort of implied, from what I remember." He breathed out, slow and steady, as if the memory was flooding him. "And I remember that moment with perfect clarity."

Oh God. Of course, he'd bring up the lake the very first time he saw her again, even if it *had* been eight years since that day. The truth settled in—Reid Malone might sound like a gentleman, but he certainly wasn't. He looked more like a hungry wolf ready to pounce, and she knew what that was about.

Kathy Newcastle had warned her, and here he was, twice in one day. On the hunt.

"I didn't plan on coming back—"

"Yet here you are," he said. "I could take this place off your hands. You can make a good profit and you wouldn't be saddled here because of some investment your dad made."

"Not for sale," she said, marveling at his nerve. What was he up to?

"Everything's for sale."

She most certainly was not for sale. "Thanks for stopping by," she snapped, distracting her anger by turning to inspect the flowers in the bed. Except for one spot she'd missed (thanks to Reid's inopportune interruption) and the vines she still needed to make climb up the columns, everything looked good.

He glanced at the beds, his eyes narrowing slightly. She held her breath, waiting to see if he'd noticed the change, but he didn't say anything.

Which filled her with relief. Maybe he didn't pay much attention to detail and hadn't noticed anything out of the ordinary that day at the lake, either.

She hurried away from the flowers, dug her keys from her pocket, and plunged one into the lock, pushing the front door open and stepping inside to the shop.

As she turned to close the door, she thought she saw that dog again. She peered at it, her senses on high alert, her heart skittering. What was it? A small retriever? No. Some sort of terrier. She didn't know why it bothered her.

She shook off the feeling of foreboding settling over her. It was just a dog. Her reaction had to be from her proximity to Reid, pure and simple. He was mortal, and he and his dad had tried to railroad her father, but none of that mattered. The air between them was charged with electricity.

The momentary distraction was enough to let Reid push through the door after her. "I'd heard you were back," he said, "but I had to see it for myself."

"*I* heard that I shouldn't trust you," she shot back. In her mind, her voice shook, her nerves rattling her to the core.

But, thankfully, to her ears, she sounded remarkably calm. Forceful, even. He was smug and cocky and had some nerve coming in here as though he had any right to. And he was too good-looking for his own britches.

Reid laughed. Actually, he took off his cowboy hat, and *then* he laughed. His mirth didn't spread from his mouth to his eyes, though. "I don't know who told you that, but you shouldn't believe everything you hear, darlin'."

"I don't, *darlin'*, unless it comes from a reliable source. And, well—" She spread her arms. "There you go."

"Who's the reliable source? Oh, no, wait. Let me guess." He stroked his chin, the side of his thumb resting against his soul patch enticingly. Why, oh why did he have to look so good?

Thankfully his acerbic personality kept her lucid.

"I'd reckon Kathy Newcastle's been talking," he said after a pause.

If he'd been paying any attention from behind the windows of The Speakeasy, it was a pretty easy job to guess it was Kathy doing the talking. Folks only stopped by to gawk, not gossip. "Guess you've been paying attention to what's been going on around here. Why so curious, Reid? Don't you have anything better to do than spy on me?"

"Guess not," he said, an amused smile playing on his lips. Full, kissable lips.

No. She banished the thought and dragged her gaze back to the deep-blue granite of his eyes, debating her options. Did she show him the door and cut the conversation off now, or play along with this little game of verbal cat-and-mouse and find out what he wanted? Oh, how she wished she could go back to hiding in the stairwell to her loft.

"Can I help you with something, Reid? I have a lot to do to get ready for the grand opening." As if to punctuate just how much, she pulled her newest list out of her back pocket and waved it in front of him.

"Nothing better to do at ten o'clock at night than work through your chores?" He shook his head. "Tsk, tsk."

Her anger flared as she peered at him. "Can I help you with something?" she repeated, resisting the urge to snap her fingers, magically lash his hands behind his back, and zip his mouth shut.

"Not right now. I was just curious." He moved toward her until the thinnest breath of air could pass between them. The air sizzled as he lifted his arm, and for a split second, she had the fantasy that he was going to slip it around her back and pull her to him as he had at the lake when he'd lifted her onto the hood of her daddy's truck. Her breath caught in her throat, but she finally released it when his hand slid along the built-in bookshelves, the freestanding units, and the tables and chairs instead of along the contours of her body.

God, what was wrong with her? She stilled her racing heart, gathering her bearings, but her thoughts took a sharp turn. He'd touched her body once before. His mouth had sucked on her nipples and his fingers had teased the heat between her legs, but he hadn't kissed her. What would it feel like to finally have his lips against hers after so many years, to have that intimacy and that connection with him, mortal or not?

As he walked through the front of the store and into the garden room, she forced her thoughts back to the café. She had indoor trees to bring in, twinkling lights, and outdoor furniture. In the winter, on cold days, people could stay inside the room, but on nice spring days, they'd open up the bay doors and spill out into the actual garden.

One more thing on her to-do list. She concentrated her thoughts, holding an imaginary pencil and writing the items in the air. They'd appear on her actual list, a bit of magic she'd discovered when she was eight years old and had scribbled in the air with her fist, angry over a nine-year-old bully who'd made fun of her. Thick black scribble marks had ended up all over his yearbook as a result.

Her mind returned to her list. She wanted to plant a garden. Or maybe conjure one. Did it even have to wait until spring?

Yes, of course it did. People would notice, and besides, she couldn't afford the energy plunge a full garden would cause her. She had too much to do each and every day to feel worn out from casting spells.

"So Buddy Garland's doing the work?"

Of course he already knew the answer, but she answered him anyway. "Yes, you know him?"

"Everybody knows him," he said. "When he doesn't have a job, he parks it at The Speakeasy and doesn't move for days."

"So I hear," she said, steering him back into the front room, and hopefully right out the front door.

He stopped short, turning to face her. She careered into him, her palm flattening against his chest. Heat flared between them. She jerked her hand away, her skin instantly turning cold once their connection was broken.

He looked down at her, his voice lowering. "You really think coming back here was a good idea?"

She stared at him. "Why wouldn't it be?"

He shrugged, but that cocky grin returned. "Because we have unfinished business."

The air between them sizzled again, but she backed away. "We have no unfinished business," she ground out, but in truth, it was all she'd thought about since she'd found out he was still here in Whiskey Creek.

He closed the distance between them again. "Oh, but we do. Ever since that day at the lake, I've had a question I wanted to ask you."

"And then you'll leave?"

"Sure, darlin', if that's what you really want."

"It is." She bolstered herself, knowing what he was going to ask, but having no idea how she would answer it.

"When we were, you know—" He paused, leaving the words hanging there and she gulped. "There wasn't a storm in the forecast, but then, suddenly, one was brewing. Why is that?"

Her blood seemed to ratchet into motion. So he *had* noticed the lightning crackling like a web of electricity across the sky. Being so close to him now, she could feel the same energy coursing through her, gushing into a pool of uncontrollable power. Oh, not good. If she didn't keep it together, she'd blow and her magic would surface, just as surely as Old Faithful. "I'm not a weather girl," she said.

His gaze slid over her as if he were making his own assessment. "No, you're a bookstore/café owner. Nothing to do with the weather."

Good. At least they got that cleared up. But damn it if he didn't stay rooted to the ground where he stood.

Waiting.

"Why were you at the lake that day?"

He wasn't going to budge until she answered; she'd bet her life on it. "My dad and I used to go to the pier at that old fishing cabin," she said. "I—I got some bad news that day. I needed to think."

His eyes narrowed. "What kind of bad news chased you out there? In the middle of a storm that wasn't supposed to happen?"

She swallowed. She'd *summoned* the storm to make herself feel better, but it hadn't worked. Neither had nearly having sex with Reid right there on the lakeshore. The way he looked made her shiver. It was as if he knew about her magic but wasn't telling. Or maybe she was just paranoid.

Her mind froze. How was she supposed to answer that? *I went to the lake to use my magic with the weather. It's the one thing I could control that day.*

Uh, no.

"What kind of news?" he asked again.

"None of your business," she snapped.

She waited for him to utter some generic apology for asking. He didn't.

What a guy.

She grabbed a stack of books from the nearest box and shoved them on the closest shelf, wishing again for that giant hook to drag him outside and far, far away from her and The Storiebook Café. "Anything else?"

He paused for a minute, as if he were contemplating the possibilities. "Now that you mention it," he said, "I have this picture of you in my head and I can't seem to get it out. I thought maybe—"

"What picture?" she said as calmly as possible, but her cheeks heated again, and her palms grew sweaty. She knew exactly what image played in his head. He was envisioning her naked. Or nearly naked.

He moved like a wolf, lithe and graceful, advancing toward her. Instinct kicked in and she backed away, but she ended up flat against one of the built-ins. Trapped.

"Oh, you know what I'm remembering," he said. "White T-shirt and what was left of your blue jeans. Mmm mmm. I can picture it like it was yesterday." His finger grazed the sleeve of her shirt. "Sopping wet, too, and pulled up just enough to—"

"Reid Malone, you just stop."

With utter control, his gaze moved from her face to her body. "Stop what, darlin'? You're not enjoying our little reunion?"

"What do you want, Reid?"

He looked at her with a heated expression that she couldn't read, almost as if what he wanted, and what he could have, were two different things. He dropped his voice. "Maybe I want you."

Her shoulders tensed. "I'm not available."

"Not even for the right price?"

She balked and bit back a laugh. Had he set out to get under her skin? "Are you propositioning me?"

He shrugged. "That list of yours is awful long. We could trade a little labor for a good time."

Her body tensed at the idea of trading anything with him. She threw her shoulders back. "My list is not that long, and I'm not that desperate. Buddy's working out just fine, thank you very much, and I'm not for sale."

He put his hat on. "That's a cryin' shame. Could have been fun."

"I get along just fine."

"You keep telling yourself that, but everyone needs a little merriment now and again, and you seem strung pretty tight."

She scowled, the energy she'd barely been controlling exploding. As quickly as she could, she concentrated on the inky sky outside so she wouldn't blow out the windows. A split second later, thunder cracked.

His attention diverted and he looked out the window. Enough of a distraction that she managed to drag in a raspy breath. "Stop picturing me. Stop thinking about me. Stop coming around," she said.

He turned back to her with a crooked grin that, damn him, ate her craw. "I don't know if I can do that, Storie. Seeing you again has conjured up some...fond memories for me."

"Not so fond for me," she said. The energy mounted, growing like a gathering wave, and then once again, a boom crashed in the sky outside.

He whipped his head around, staring through the window. "What the hell?"

She put her hands on his chest, ignoring the hard muscles underneath the cotton and the heat emanating from him. Ignored the zing and zap that felt like she'd just been shocked.

She gave him a forced smile as another crash of thunder sounded. "You're conjuring up memories for me, too, sugar, only they're not ones I want to experience again, so unless you have some other business here, you can go."

"Now that you mention it," he said casually, "I thought I might take a look at Buddy's handiwork."

Now they were getting down to the truth of the matter. He definitely wanted something, and it wasn't to relive their night at the lake. "Why'd you want to buy this place, Reid? Looking to expand your bar?"

He laughed. "Not even close. My dad—" His jaw tightened. "Never mind. So you're not going to let me look around?"

"No."

One of his eyebrows arched. "No?"

Like a mirror, she arched one of hers in response. "*Hell*, no."

"My, my," he said with a wry grin, "such hostility."

Said the wolf to Little Red Riding Hood. "My, my," she said, matching his sardonic smile, "such a player."

And then she gave him a good hard shove backward, using just enough magic to direct him out the door. Once he was clear of the threshold, she waved her hand, slamming the door with an invisible force and throwing the deadbolt.

"And stay away," she said under her breath.

CHAPTER 4

A SIX-SHOOTER. There was no other way to describe Storie Bell. The woman was packing all kinds of gunpowder, and he'd just unleashed the smallest dusting of it. Tormenting her while he figured out how to search the building just might be the most fun he'd have for years to come.

If it didn't get him into a whole heap of trouble first.

He stepped behind the bar at The Speakeasy and poured himself a draft before leaning against the mahogany countertop.

She'd pushed him out of her café, and his chest still burned from the heat of her hands. And those eyes. They were as green as the hills in May when everything was fresh and the rain was falling. Emerald and lush, they'd bored into him as if she could read him just as easily as she could read one of the books on the shelves of the store.

But mostly, it had been the fire that almost sparked from her fingertips and hovered on the tip of her tongue that intrigued him and had caused a longing to resurface, a longing that he hadn't thought he'd ever feel again. What would it feel like to have that tongue slipping between his lips...

Ah hell, if he wasn't careful, he'd be telling her all about Gemstone Spirits and the Apple Pie Moonshine recipe. He'd hand the thing over if she asked him to with those lips.

"That was quick, baby," Jules said, trailing her finger up his arm. "Came to your senses, did you?"

His good mood faded.

"Never lost 'em, Jules," he said, sidestepping her. He wished he hadn't lost them six months ago when he'd spent the night with her. She'd been working him over the coals ever since, trying hard to get back into his bed. She was nice enough, and yeah, she'd made him happy for a night. But he wanted out of Whiskey Creek—not something else to keep him here, not that Jules was the person who could do that, anyway. But still, the fewer attachments he had, the easier it would be to leave one day.

"Get what you were after?" she asked, going back to drying the tall bar glasses.

"Not yet," he said, "but I will." Now that he'd seen Storie again, after however many years it had been—eight?—all his old desires had flooded to the surface again. No one compared to her. But she was back, and he was on his way out.

Timing...and property ownership...were everything.

He'd hardly had a chance to look around her shop, and the light had been dim. He'd had every intention of making nice, ingratiating himself to Storie so he could snoop more easily, but Christ almighty, the woman was stubborn and difficult. He needed a different plan if he was going to get back into the café to look around. Clearly, she hadn't been taken with his charm.

Or maybe he would always be persona non grata to her

after their encounter at the lake, an event she probably wanted to pretend had never happened.

"But it did happen," he said under his breath as he plotted his next move. He'd get what he needed—and maybe what he wanted—and Storie Bell would never be the wiser.

* * *

Reid Malone's challenge and infuriating attitude had shaken her, and now not even the sound of Harper singing to herself in the kitchen gave Storie a bit of comfort. Outside, not a single leaf fluttered on the trees, and the humid air was stifling. But inside the café, Storie blasted the air conditioner and the music as she unpacked boxes, logged new inventory, and shelved books. She was trying hard to forget about her encounter with Reid the night before, but it wasn't working.

She didn't trust him; that was the bottom line. She couldn't put her finger on why.

If he'd shown up a minute earlier than he had—or even thirty seconds sooner—he'd have seen her doing magic, but part of her wondered if he had seen and just wasn't letting on.

Of course he'd already seen it, although maybe he didn't realize it.

Harper rattled around in the kitchen, organizing the pots and pans, spices and herbs, and the nonperishables in the pantry. The books and the store itself were under Storie's purview, and the kitchen belonged to Harper.

"You girls go on out to play," Harper said, shooing Scarlett and Piper out of the kitchen and through the front door. "Go on down to the creamery and get yourselves an ice cream." She handed them a few dollars and they scampered away.

There was no sign of the contractor, though there was

evidence he'd been there working. A ladder was propped up against the built-in bookshelf behind them. A smattering of footprints tracked through the sawdust on the concrete floor. A circular saw lay smack in the middle of the garden room.

Throw rugs. They needed throw rugs. Storie added them to her list. She'd need plenty of them until she and Harper could paint the floor in the outdoor room with the black-and-white diamond pattern they'd agreed on.

All of which just reminded her of everything she had to do, which made her think of Buddy Garland and his handyman work, which brought up Reid again, and all she could think of was his insistence that they had unfinished business.

She tried to keep perspective. No mortal men. A relationship with one would never work, assuming she'd even want it to. Which she didn't. Add to that the fact that she didn't know any warlocks or wizards, and her fate was sealed. There would be no merriment and love in her future.

A few minutes later, she and Harper stood side by side. Storie finished telling her friend what Reid had said, and Harper stared at her as if she'd grown horns. "He said that?" she whispered. "That everything's for sale?"

Storie nodded grimly as she pulled her hair into a ponytail, winding a bright orange hair band around the mass. "But let me tell you, he's got another thing coming. He wants something, but I am not for sale. He can't waltz in here and think I'll barter with him." She scoffed. "He made it sound like he'd help get us ready for the grand opening if we finished that…business at the lake."

"You mean the sex you almost had, but didn't," Harper said, winking.

"Yes, that's what I mean."

"I might," Harper said. "He's hot."

Storie flung the back of her hand against Harper's arm. "That's not the point."

"Could be."

Storie shook her head. "He may be gorgeous, but that's not enough," she said.

"To you," Harper said with a laugh. "For me, it's more than enough."

Buddy Garland appeared, interrupting their conversation. The long strands of his sparse iron-gray hair flew toward the ceiling, his leathery skin covered with a fine layer of dust.

"Ladies," he said.

A little dog trotted in behind him, looking up at them with big, round eyes.

Behind her, Miranda hissed.

"Where'd he come from?" Harper asked. But Storie's skin pricked. It was the same dog she'd seen across the road at the courthouse square.

Buddy shrugged. "Followed me in this mornin'. He's a friendly thing."

Harper crouched and held out her hand. "Come here, boy." The dog barked, but scampered toward her. She peeked under the terrier's back leg. "I mean girl," she amended with a laugh.

They turned their attention back to Buddy as he cleared his throat.

"The fence out back is finished," he proclaimed, as if that was the final repair job and they were ready to open. Which they definitely were not.

Storie pulled her list out of her back pocket and peered at it. "What about the shelves in the tearoom and fixing the motor on the garage door opener?"

Buddy shrugged, bending down to pick up the circular

saw. "Didn't get to 'em yet," he said, "and I got another job I gotta start up now."

Storie gaped at him. "What do you mean, you have another job? You're still on *this* job."

Buddy shrugged and went about his business, gathering up the rest of his tools. "Money talks, little lady, and I been paid real handsomely to take another job."

"Buddy," she said, working to slow her manic pulse, "we have a grand opening coming next week."

"Bad timing," he admitted.

She and Harper stared. "Are you kidding? Bad timing?" Storie's fists clenched, all the energy inside of her swirling into an uncontrollable frenzy. "You can't leave."

"You can't stop me," he said, but he wouldn't make eye contact. Her senses went on high alert. Something wasn't right.

"Oh yes, I can stop you," she ground out. "We have a contract."

"This other job's a biggie."

Harper threw out one hip and propped her arms on it. "What exactly are you telling us, Buddy Garland? You have a biggie job right here."

"Yes, ma'am, but this new one's *bigger*."

Storie wagged her finger at him. "Oh no, Buddy. We were just telling Kathy Newcastle what a find you were. You can't leave us high and dry and make us all liars."

"I can't help it if somethin' has come up," he said, still not meeting her eyes.

Storie suddenly thought of Reid and Jiggs Malone trying to buy this place from her dad, of Reid showing up and trying to barter work for sex, and then she remembered Kathy telling her that Buddy parked himself at The Speakeasy when he wasn't working. Oh God. Surely Reid wouldn't... Would he? Could he possibly be *that* duplicitous?

She kept her voice calm, but her blood surged like a hurricane in her ears. "Did Reid Malone put you up to this?"

Buddy stuttered, speechless, and that was all she needed to know.

The reality of what it meant set in. For a moment, she couldn't see straight. Couldn't think. Kathy had been right. The man couldn't be trusted, but if he thought stealing Buddy Garland away from them would stop anything, he was dead wrong.

She hadn't fallen into rapture at seeing him again, hadn't succumbed to his so-called charm—so he was going to sabotage her business. Maybe he didn't want the actual business. Maybe this was payback for eight-year-old sexual frustration, ridiculous as that was.

Buddy brushed down the wayward strands of his hair, looking a touch uncomfortable. "Don't fret none, Ms. Bell. I got you covered. My word is gold. Your list'll get done in time for your opening by the end of this week."

"How can it, if you're leaving?" she asked, wondering how, if she used magic, she was going to explain the work being done to Harper.

He stopped at the archway leading back to the front of the store. "My word is gold," he said again. "Everythin' will get done."

Harper jammed her hands on her hips, staring him down with a look so intense, Storie thought that if she had magic in her, Mr. Garland would have been turned into a rat by now. "How can it be?" she hollered after him. "There's still this room to finish, the cupboards in the kitchen, and you haven't even started working on the apartment upstairs—"

Storie waved that task away. The upstairs loft was truly the last priority, but in the meantime, she was living in squalor. Magic was not an option for that. Harper, the girls, Buddy, and Kathy Newcastle had all seen it, and they'd ask too many questions if it was suddenly fixed up, so she'd have to continue living out of boxes for as long as it took.

Buddy gave them a curt nod as he headed out the front door. "It'll get done," he said again, but Storie had lost faith. So far, being in Whiskey Creek didn't feel like happily ever after. And seeing Reid again had made everything take a turn for the worse. Her father's words circled in her mind again. Mortals and witches didn't mix.

Before they could argue another word with the wayward contractor, he was gone.

Only the little dog stayed behind.

CHAPTER 5

REID WOULD BET his life that bootleggers and moonshiners were not what Storie'd had in mind when she dreamed up The Storiebook Café. He'd also bet that his arrangement with Buddy Garland to bail on the job next door had her blowing steam out of her ears. He'd timed it just right—wait long enough to make her and Harper sweat, but not so long that they'd go off and hire another contractor to do the work.

Deceiving Storie might not be honorable, but it was fun. And truthfully, he was trying to protect her and Harper. Probable deniability. What they didn't know couldn't hurt them. Or get them tossed in prison.

Twenty-four hours. He figured that was enough.

"You gotta hang the cupboard doors in the kitchen," Buddy said. He dug his hand into a wooden bowl of peanuts and popped a few into his mouth. "Then there're the built-in bookshelves. They're in the tearoom for the little 'uns. A few of the shelves are warped, is all. I'd leave that for last. The upstairs needs a lot of work. Ms. Bell can't move in fully till it's done, but she said that can wait till last. Floor needs refinishing. Needs new countertops in the kitchenette and new drywall."

Why he even bothered making notes of everything Buddy mentioned, he didn't know. He had no intention of actually *doing* the bulk of the repairs. Some of them, sure. He needed access to search, and that was it. Get in, get out. It was as simple as that.

And if he could loosen those springs wound up inside Storie and taste her again, all the better.

He nodded his thanks to Buddy for taking the fall, handed over an ancient bottle of Jiggs's moonshine, gathered up his tools, and five minutes later he pushed through the front door of the bookshop ready for a throwdown with Storie.

But instead of Storie, the two little girls he'd seen flitting around the square and darting in and out of the shop stared up at him. Harper's daughters. They both hung back. He waved at them, giving them a friendly smile.

The younger girl folded her arms and stared him down, but eventually she spoke. "Are you Prince Charming or a bandit?"

He set down the toolbox he'd lugged over. Kids. It wasn't that he didn't like them; he just didn't know how to relate to them. At least it was an easy question. The corner of his mouth crept up. "Probably closer to a bandit."

"Well then, you shouldn't be here." The older girl spoke this time, hands on her hips. He bit back a chuckle. She was the spitting image of her mama, and she'd definitely have the boys lining up for her one day.

"I'm a *good* bandit," he said, and it was the truth. He was only trying to do right by Jiggs. But he was also a stranger to them, he realized. A mad rush of grumbling drowned out the music streaming from the cutout in the wall leading to the kitchen. "Can I talk to your mama?" He knew it wouldn't be easy to convince Storie that he was there to help. Since she didn't appear to be here, he'd work on Harper. They had no history, so maybe she'd see that his motives were true.

The older girl tipped her chin down and peered up at him. Without taking her eyes off him, she called out. "Mama!" She shoved the little girl toward the kitchen. "Scarlett, go get Mama."

Scarlett obeyed, scampering off, and three seconds later, Harper appeared, wiping her hands on a ruffled apron tied around her waist. She peered at him, her gaze snapping to the toolbox he'd set down, then back to him. Maybe she wouldn't be any easier to convince. "Reid Malone, if I'm not mistaken," she said.

He touched the bill of his Rangers cap. "At your service."

"And what can I do for you?"

"Cut to the chase. I like that." He smiled, rocking back on his heels. "I thought Buddy told you—"

"Told me what?" she said, throwing one leg out and propping a hand on her hip. One eye narrowed, her eyebrows arching into a V. He looked down at the girls and stifled a laugh. They were three peas in a pod, each of them in the exact same position, staring at him with the exact same expression.

"That I'd be filling in. Said you had to have the place finished by the opening."

"Right. That's Friday."

He spread his arms wide. "So here I am. Just wanted to do my part to help. Couldn't leave you high and dry."

"Is that right?" she asked, her lips drawing into a tight bow. "We got the feeling he left because of you."

"Me?" So maybe his plan wasn't as foolproof as he'd hoped. "No, he just took another job."

She hesitated. "Well, he did say his word was gold, but—"

"Yep, that's right. Buddy's as good as they come," he said.

And that was the truth. This wasn't like a pro ball player throwing the championship game. Moonshine went a long way toward convincing a man like Buddy to give up a job. Not that he'd tell Harper that.

She hesitated for a second, looking over her shoulder. Was she hoping Storie would show up? He wouldn't mind seeing her again, too, stubbornness and all. He needed to strategize on where to start his work here, but having her in his sights would be a bonus, as long as he could search without her being the wiser.

Then again, if she was pissed off at him, he could search without her being a distraction. He honestly didn't know which scenario he preferred.

Finally, Harper nodded. "Okay then," she said. "There's a list around here somewhere. It's about as long as my arm." She scurried off to the kitchen, returning a few minutes later with a yellow legal pad. Neat, straight-up-and-down script filled sheet after sheet. "Storie's a list-maker," she explained. "She has it all written down, in multiple places. You can start at the top and work your way down. The air conditioner just went kaput, too, so that'll be added on."

He took the pad, scanning the to-do tasks.

- *Fix the clog in the kitchen sink*
- *Warped shelving in tearoom*
- *Bent paneling in garage*
- *Broken light fixture in front*
- *Railings on garage doors*
- *Paint cupboards in kitchen*
- *Pantry light*

STORIEBOOK CHARM

The list went on and on, ending with a second page detailing what needed to be done in the apartment upstairs. The thing was at least four times as long as Buddy had led him to believe. Good God, he had his own list of things to do at The Speakeasy. Best he get on with his search and get the hell out of here.

But where to start? Hell, it might help if he knew exactly what he was looking for. The best Jiggs could tell him was that the secret ingredient was an oil, and vital to the moonshine recipe that Gemstone wanted to buy. Problem was, only Ted Bell knew what it was, and he was dead. But Reid had been in and out of here enough times to know that nothing was hidden in plain sight, and now he was desperate. The deal had to be inked or Jiggs wouldn't make his millions and find his peace of mind.

Whatever kind of receptacle the oil was in, he was determined to find it. If only the building weren't so old. There was no telling where Storie's father might have hidden the special stuff. If there was any more of it. That's what worried Reid most of all. What if Ted had given Jiggs the last of the elixir? It had a distinct flavor and they hadn't been able to replicate it. Without it, Jiggs's moonshine was nothing special, but with it, the stuff was a gold mine.

"Don't need to bother with upstairs right now," Harper said. "All the downstairs stuff is the priority."

He picked up his tools, a sliver of remorse slicing into his thinking. He wasn't a Boy Scout, but he wasn't dishonest, yet here he was trying to find and steal something that didn't belong to him.

"How long did Storie's dad own this place?"

"Ever since I've known her. Since she was a senior in high school, I reckon. Can't believe he never fixed it up," she said, "but it's been a clean slate for us, which is good. This is the town they lived in when her parents first split up. It's like he knew she'd end up here."

"Bet he had a bunch of junk in here, eh?"

"Nah, place was pretty clean, surprisingly." She headed back to the kitchen. "There's a heap of stuff in the side yard, but that's about it. Old wood and probably a hotbed of scorpions. Hauling it away is on the list."

The side yard. He thought about moving that task to the top of his list, but decided against it. Little vials of infused oil or whatever the secret ingredient was wouldn't be in the junk pile outside.

For now he'd start downstairs and work his way through the building. If his search downstairs didn't uncover anything, he'd have to figure out how to get upstairs into Storie's loft.

His brain grew hazy at the very idea of getting that close to her again, and the doubts about what he was doing crowded back to the front of his mind. He didn't like deceiving Storie, but he didn't know how else to get what his dad needed, and right or wrong, Jiggs needed his help. He picked up his tools, looked at the list of things to do, and headed off to the tearoom. It was as good a place as any to start, and since he was here searching, he might as well help. A little, anyway.

CHAPTER 6

THE AFTERNOON WAS hotter than a two-dollar pistol, but the blistering heat was instantly forgotten as Storie stepped into the shop. The air conditioner wasn't blasting cold air through the café. The damn thing went on the fritz and was now on the list of things to fix. She was beyond tempted to wave her hand, utter a spell, and fix the thing herself. Instead, she scrawled with an invisible pencil, adding to the lengthy list they already had going.

Rumblings around town were one thing, but out-and-out blatant witchcraft, that was something else.

If it came right down to it, though, she'd already decided she'd send Harper away for an afternoon and fix everything herself, saying she'd found the most amazing contractor to take over for Buddy.

The door opened behind her. She turned, ready to greet a potential new customer. Instead she was met with a trembling mail woman. She hurried in and dropped the stack of catalogs and letters on the first table she came to.

"Thanks." Storie held her hand out and stepped forward, but her smile froze on her lips when the woman didn't answer. The woman threw up her hand in a quick wave and darted back out the door, leaving Storie staring at her empty shop.

So Storie's reputation hadn't faded. In an instant, all the anxiety she'd felt as a child as her magic had gone haywire pooled in her gut. Her hope started to ebb as she realized that she might be destined to never fit in anywhere.

She tried to let the incident go as she heard the sweet sound of a hammer pounding against wood. Maybe she wouldn't have to go so far as to cast spells around Harper and the girls, because Buddy was back.

She passed the kitchen, glancing in to see Harper as she worked in the pantry organizing supplies. Two thin cords hung down from her ears and her shoulders moved to the music playing from her iPod. The girls perched on stools at the bistro table that was pushed against the side wall.

They looked up from their coloring. Scarlett wiggled in her seat and chirped, "There's a bandit in there!"

Storie grinned. Buddy the bandit. At least he was a bandit with a heart. "So I hear." She flipped her hand up in a quick wave and followed the pounding to the tearoom.

"You came back—" She stumbled at the threshold. The slant of the shoulders. The way the supple cotton of his smoky blue T-shirt draped down his back. The fit of his jeans. Oh lord, that was *not* Buddy Garland. It was Reid Malone. "What are you doing?"

His momentum slowed as he hit the hammer against the underside of a shelf in the built-in unit. His body stilled, the muscles tensing under his shirt as he turned to face her. Deliberate. Unhurried. Bandit-like.

"Just helping out," he said with a slow, sultry drawl that would melt any girl's heart. Any girl except Storie. "Heard Buddy had to stop working here to go to another project. Thought I'd fill in for him." He pointed to the floor.

"We don't need you to fill in," she said. Complete lie, but she didn't want him in the café with his seductive smile and cowboy charm.

He looked at her for a long few seconds before nodding. "If you say so. Guess you have someone else to get all the work done on that list of yours."

She followed the direction he pointed. A yellow legal pad was on the floor. He glanced at it, and she could have sworn his body stilled even more.

The busted air conditioner. Crap. She'd used magic to put it on the to-do list. Had he realized there was a new task added?

If he did, he kept quiet, finally raising his gaze back to hers, and said, "Might want to confer with Harper. She gave the okay." He bent down and began to pack up his tools.

"Dammit." On the one hand, she didn't want him anywhere near her. He irritated the hell out of her, and she knew he had some agenda. She just didn't know what that agenda was. But on the other hand, she and Harper needed the work done.

"Stop," she said.

He turned to her, his lips curving into a taunting smile. "Stop, please?"

She blinked. Stared. And sucked in a calming breath. "Stop, *please*," she ground out.

He gave a long-suffering sigh, making slow, deliberate work of unpacking the tools. "Since you asked so nicely."

She seethed inside, but her hands were tied. Even if he was responsible for them losing Buddy, she needed him…at least for the moment.

"There's a lot to do before you open. You should be working, too."

She chased away her frustration and focused on the situation in front of her. "What do you think I've been doing?"

He looked up at her, his eyes boring into her. "Planting flowers?"

She barely resisted stomping her foot in indignation. Because while she might not have followed the traditional route, she had made flowers grow. Still, she wasn't lying when she said, "No, I have *not* been planting flowers."

He gave her a long, intent stare. "So how do you explain all those colorful things overflowing in the front beds, and all those bundles drying in the stairwell? Looks like you've been doing nothing *but* gardening."

She bristled under his scrutiny, taking a step backward. Was his observation innocent, or was he trying to tell her that he knew they hadn't been planted the old-fashioned way? "I can garden quickly, and I've been doing plenty of other things," she said. "Like taking inventory, stocking, organizing, setting up the accounting system."

He frowned, his eyebrows pulling together. "Uh-huh."

"So where did Buddy really go?" she asked, changing the subject and getting down to the question burning in her mind. Buddy didn't set her off-kilter or make her nerves twine. Reid did, and then some. "Or did *you* have something to do with him leaving us in the lurch?"

The corner of his mouth lifted in a smile and he looked at her as though he was ready to devour every inch of her. "Me?" he asked innocently. Or as innocently as a man with taut biceps, a little bit of a tattoo showing under his sleeve, and a soul patch could. "Why would I do something like that?"

She started to answer, but thought better of it. None of the scenarios were good, so she kept quiet.

"Don't think too hard on it, darlin'. Buddy got a better offer, and I had a few hours to spare so here I am. I'm just helping out a friend."

Helping out himself was more like it. He'd once gotten a

pretty good sample of what was underneath her clothes. Now she bristled under his gaze, feeling exposed.

Was it possible that she was completely wrong? Was her embarrassment over that moment together so long ago coloring her perception of him? The truth was, since Buddy wasn't here and the grand opening was looming, she did need Reid. "Full disclosure, Reid," she said, nearly biting back the words before they left her mouth. But once they were out, she couldn't pull them back.

He angled his gaze down at her. "Okay."

"Why are you really here? I know you're not just helping out Buddy...or Harper and me. So what is it you want?"

He gave her that half-cocked grin again. "Full disclosure?"

She nodded. Not that she expected him to be completely straight, but even the partial truth would be something.

He paused, as though he was weighing his options, and then he said, "Like I told you before, I think we could have a little fun together. I'm a businessman. Bartering. Trading. I scratch your back, you scratch mine. Unfinished business, Storie. That's what I want...*if* we're being honest."

She balked, stepping forward, resisting the temptation to jab her finger against his chest to drive her anger home. "So let me get this straight. You thought stepping in to pick up where Buddy left off might make me so grateful that I'd sleep with you?"

He shrugged. "You make it sound so sinister."

She took a page out of Harper's book of indignation and propped one hand on her hip. "Isn't it?"

He tilted his head, that smirk firmly on his face. "No, it's fun. F.U.N. Ever heard of it?"

"Kathy was right," she said, not sure why she was so surprised. She'd hoped that she was wrong and that Reid wasn't as self-serving as she feared.

"Oh yeah? About what?"

"She said I should watch out for you."

"Too much hairspray will make a woman nutty," he said.

"I think she's right on target."

"You're a little untrusting, aren't you, Storiebook?"

Her spine stiffened at the nickname her dad used to call her, but brushed it off. "I'm plenty trusting with people who've earned it."

"What does that mean? You trust Harper? Her daughters?"

She nodded. "Exactly."

"Uh-huh." He folded his arms across his chest. "Anybody else, or does that about cover it? Any more friends hiding around here?"

She took a step back, the sting of his words making her feel as if she'd been slapped. How could he know how alone in the world she was, and why would he drive the point home like that? The swirling sensation sparking in her felt dark and concentrated. She fisted her hands and it grew until it pooled low in her belly.

His smile was taunting. "Since I'm not to be trusted, I guess I'll just get back to work, darlin'." His jaw tensed as he turned back to the shelves and set his hammer down gently. He angled himself up against the unit, placed both hands underneath, and shoved with all his might.

The shelf didn't budge.

She bit her lip, trying to hold in mirth bubbling up in her throat. "Buddy popped the last one off like he was flipping a light switch," she said, only mildly bothered at how much pleasure she took in his failure.

Reid shot her a look that made her squirm. "Did he now?"

"Yes, he did."

He just scowled under his breath, readied himself, and shoved up against the shelf again. It jarred, but still stuck.

That shelf, she decided right then and there, wasn't going

anywhere. His back was turned to her so she flicked her hand, pointing her index finger toward him. A faint glow swirled around her fingertips from the magic. As he turned, she quickly tucked her hand behind her back.

He scowled, rooted his feet, and shoved again, this time bending his knees and thrusting upward with his shoulder, grunting.

The shelf held firm.

"What the—?" He cursed under his breath, his frustration palpable.

"Carpentry is hard work. I'm sure I can find someone more qualified," she said sweetly. "I mean, you're not used to manual labor. Boxes of beer, that's probably the extent of your heavy lifting behind the bar."

He tossed the hammer, spinning it around by the handle in his hand. His neck muscles strained, pulsing, but after a moment and a deep breath, his voice was calm. "You gained a sense of humor since I saw you last."

She bit back a laugh. Her jabs at him had started out of anger, but he was pretty fun to tease, as it turned out. "You bring out the best in me, what can I say?"

He smirked, as if he wasn't so sure that what she was exhibiting was her best. "I helped renovate that bar, so I'd say I'm plenty qualified," he shot back.

She gave a slow, pointed look at the stubborn shelf. "If you say so."

His face tense, he leaned against the unit, seeming to let his anger go. He crossed one leg over the other and folded his arms over his chest. "From what I hear, the upstairs needs some work. Wanna give me a personal tour?"

She tried to swallow around the tangle of nerves lodged in her throat. Reid Malone in her apartment? Near her bed? Her heart raced at the visual. Not in a million years. She didn't want him down here, let alone upstairs. That was definitely off-limits.

She wanted to settle down, and falling for a bad-boy wanderer who was, quite frankly, an ass, wasn't part of the plan.

"Some other time," she said just as a gust of swirling wind blew through the little tearoom from the front. Her magic was working without her even trying. Oh boy. Maybe he was bringing out the worst in her. Mortal men. "Not," she said, just loud enough for him to hear.

"Don't be so sure about that," he said. "I have a way of wearing women down so I can do what needs to be done."

She froze, blinking away the fog filtering from her brain to her eyes. She got the feeling he knew exactly what would wear her down, and he might also know just what she needed, more than she did.

CHAPTER 7

STORIE WIELDED a brand-new black-handled carving knife in the air. "You could have called me, Harper! Or texted!" Anything to alert her to the fact that Reid would be here every day until the grand opening. She knew she was deflecting her emotions, lashing out at Harper instead of at Reid, but she couldn't stop herself.

Harper lurched back. "Hey, watch it with that thing! You're gonna take an eye out."

Storie froze for a second, glancing at the shiny blade in her hand. "Preferably Reid Malone's," she said, brandishing it again until it pointed in the direction of the tearoom where he pounded away. "Seriously, how long does it take to fix some warped shelves?"

"Longer than five minutes. Give the guy a break. At least he's here. He has his own business, plus about a bazillion dollars, so it's not like he needs to finish our renovations for us. We owe him."

Right. She pressed her fist to her forehead, the blade sticking straight up toward the ceiling. "Mineral rights," she said to herself, remembering what Kathy Newcastle had told her.

"Right, Barnett Shale."

"And he has the bar." She looked at Harper. "So why is he here?"

"Shoot," Harper said, "when Buddy's not working, he's next door parked on a barstool. Maybe another job really did come up for Buddy, and Reid's just helping out a friend. Southern kindness."

"No. He's after something. I feel it in my bones."

"And your bones are never wrong." Harper skirted around the center cutting island, ducking as she sidled up, then grabbed Storie's wrist and gently took the knife from her death grip.

Like taking the blade would stop her from derailing Reid Malone. Sure, he could probably destroy her in a surprise full frontal assault, but to fight back, she wouldn't need a knife. She just needed a flick of her wrist, or focus and a quick spell, and he'd be annihilated.

No contest.

But she couldn't do any annihilating until she knew what he was after.

Harper studied her. "You're a little distracted. You sure you're okay? Maybe you actually like having Reid here?" She flashed a suggestive smile. "It's been a while since you dated anyone, and we've already established that the man is hot."

She shot Harper a *gimme a break* look. When he watched at her, she felt exposed, as if he knew things about her. And him knowing things about her would never work. "I'm fine," she said, "and no, I don't want him here, but I know we need the help."

"If you say so," Harper said. She smiled like she knew better as she ambled out of the kitchen and gathered up

Piper and Scarlett. "See you in the morning," she called, heading out for the night.

"'Bye!" the girls called.

Storie waved them off and watched them drive away. She locked up and leaned against the door, her shoulders sagging. She couldn't tell Harper how she felt, how drained she'd gotten after growing the flowers and using her magic to do little things around the shop.

For all his faults, she missed her dad. Sure, Harper and the girls were like family, but she had never told Harper the whole truth about who she was. She was alone. This would be her life: no real family. No true connection to another person—witch, mortal, or otherwise. And no children of her own.

"If you're tired already—"

She yelped, clutching her hand to her heart. "Reid!" She caught her breath. "I didn't know…I forgot…you were still here."

"Too much to do to quit early." He held out the yellow legal pad. "Long list."

She glanced at the clock hanging on the wall near the kitchen window. "It's ten thirty."

He leaned in the threshold to the kitchen. "Got nothing better to do. Did you eat today?"

Had she? The day had started early with another shipment of books and curios, the delivery of the computer, and a training session on how to use the bar-code scanner. She and Harper had discussed menus for the next month.

"Does coffee count?" she finally asked.

"Doesn't fit into any part of the food pyramid," he said.

She laughed. "How do you know about the food pyramid?"

"This may be Podunk Whiskey Creek, but we still get occasional updates from the USDA."

Podunk Whiskey Creek—her dream town. "I guess you do."

"You okay?"

She put her hand to her growling stomach. He'd planted a seed, and now she was starving. Too bad she couldn't just conjure up some crispy french fries, and maybe a chocolate shake. Her stomach rumbled again. "Hungrier than I realized."

"The clock's ticking," he said. "Time's almost up."

She blinked, staring at him. "What did you say?"

He pulled out his phone and dialed. "You need to keep your strength up."

"I'm sure you have beer to pour or drinks to mix." She moved to unlock the door.

He was next to her in a flash, his hand on hers, turning the key to the left, the deadbolt slipping back into place. "Actually, I don't."

He started talking into his cell as he disappeared into the kitchen. She heard drawers opening and closing, the clatter of metal, and the *ping* of glass against glass. A moment later, he was spreading out a quilt he'd taken from a rack in the tearoom, and laying down napkins, silverware, and two empty glasses.

"Looks good." She sat, and once again wished she could use her magic to make a meal appear. Why was he being so nice? Her radar went off, but she was suddenly too hungry to care. "Harper'll shoot us both if we mess anything up in her kitchen. There might be some cold cereal, though."

He leveled his gaze at her, the message crystal clear. Cold cereal was not on the menu. "Try again."

"We don't have anything—?" She stopped when she heard a *tap-tap-tap* on the glass of the front door.

Reid answered, returning a second later holding a tray

laden with covered dishes with one hand, gripping a blender with the other.

"This is a little better than cold cereal," he said. He slid the tray onto the top of one of the center, freestanding bookshelves. "I had the cook at The Speakeasy whip up some burgers and fries."

"French fries?" she asked, as if there were another kind.

"Crispy, and with ketchup."

"Mmm." Exactly what she needed. And wanted. She was reluctantly impressed that he'd ordered just the right thing.

Next, he picked up the glasses and poured from the blender.

Ah, here it was. She knew it was too good to be true. The margarita. Or the daiquiri.

Something to get her liquored up, lower her resistance, and get whatever it was he was after.

"Chocolate shake," he said, handing her a frosty glass.

"No thanks—wait, what?" She stared. No way.

"Chocolate shake." He frowned. "What, you prefer a malt?"

"No, I…" She thought he'd try to ply her with alcohol, but he'd gone for her sweet tooth, as if he'd read her mind.

She took the glass, wrapping her lips around the straw, and sucked, a soft moan escaping as the thick ice cream slipped onto her tongue and down her throat. God, that was good.

She stood with her back against a shelf, watching him as he removed the domed metal plate covers and set the plates down on the quilt. He knew his way around food and she took a minute to savor the details. Before long he was sure to say or do something to raise a red flag or get her spitting mad. She certainly never thought they'd be sharing a meal like this, and that his acerbic personality would let up enough for her to actually enjoy it.

But it seemed Reid Malone had a soft side. She looked him over, smiling to herself. His soft side did *not* include the rock-hard abs she detected under his T-shirt, or the firm, muscled legs and the perfect shape of his behind under his jeans. Even his hands were strong. Capable. Her mind wandered and suddenly she was imagining those clever hands roaming her body, touching her, teasing her, and bringing her to—

"Earth to Storie."

She blinked. The image popped, but the gathering heat in her belly mounted. "What?"

"You're losing it." He pushed her plate toward her. "You need to eat."

* * *

Reid sat opposite Storie, unable to take his eyes off her. She left the burger and went straight for the fries, but it was the way she puckered her lips around the straw, her cheeks drawing in as she sucked the thick shake up, moaning as the cold ice cream finally exploded into her mouth.

He was frozen. Immobile. The image of her working that straw brought to mind something entirely luscious and sexual. Her mouth on him, that husky moan growing deeper as he flipped her over and sank himself into her. Blood pulsed from his head straight to his groin.

He fisted his hands, slowing his breath to stay in control. She took another drink. She was lost in the pleasure, and he was going to have a nervous breakdown.

Clearly, she had no idea the effect drinking a milkshake was having on him. Would have on any man. "You like that, huh?" His voice strained from the desire coursing through him.

Her eyes flew open and she met his gaze. Instantly, she released the straw, her cheeks coloring as if she realized the implications of what she'd been doing. "Sorry. I didn't mean to—"

He took another clarifying breath, his gaze dropping to her lips, before saying, "What?"

Her eyes skittered around nervously. Instead of answering, she picked up her hamburger and took a big bite. She sat cross-legged, looking anywhere but at him, as if she thought that somehow diminished how damned sexy she looked. She could be plastered in pages from a book and look good. No, she'd look freaking fantastic. Hell, she'd rock anything she put on—that was a fact—but there was something about the jeans and white tank top that drove him wild. Had ever since he'd seen her at the lake.

She swallowed, turning her head as she took a quick sip of her shake. He bit back his laugh. As if her turning away could erase the image of her lips around that damn straw and the soft, enticing sounds she made. They were burned into his brain.

She focused on her french fries, drawing her plate closer. "Why do you want out of Whiskey Creek so badly?"

He shrugged. "I like the city."

She peered up at him, frowning. "But your dad's here. The Speakeasy. And from what I hear, you have a lot of money from your mineral holdings. Isn't that enough?"

He contemplated the question, taking a drink of his own shake to wash down the last of his burger. "My mother never thought so."

She bit off a harsh laugh. "Mothers aren't always right."

That was a lot of animosity seeping into her words, but he bided his time, not wanting to spoil the moment quite yet. "Mine hated being trapped here."

She shook her head, looking completely puzzled. "I guess one person's entrapment is another's paradise."

He laughed, turning his scrutiny to her again, seizing the opening to change the subject. "Can't say as I've ever looked at it quite like that, but yeah, guess you're right."

"So what happened?"

"She fell in love with my dad, but she grew to despise him because he was small-town, and there was no brainwashing him out of that. He loves his bar, fishing at the lake, ice cream on the square. Hell, he still *is* small-town."

"And you're more like her than him," she said, nodding.

She made it sound so simple, but it wasn't. He'd grown up here and he loved all the things his father did, but he'd been drawn to the energy of the city, going off to college in Austin and practically living on Sixth Street. He'd made millions by buying up gas and mineral rights. Sweeping a woman off her feet was easy. Finding the person who wanted the same things as him wasn't. "Not necessarily. But I don't think Whiskey Creek is enough, you know?"

Storie placed another fry in her mouth, and took another sip of her drink.

His senses charged again. Everything she did seemed to affect him this way. She was distracted and wasn't thinking, he realized. "You don't like the city?" he said, hoping conversation would steady him. "This is enough for you?"

She stopped sucking her drink, seeming to ponder his question. "Absolutely."

That wasn't enough of an answer for him. He could see someone like Jules, who'd never known anything else, just never leaving a place like Whiskey Creek. Staying was easy. But his mother had lived in Dallas. She'd lived in Tucson. Now she lived in California. She knew what else was out there, and so did Storie. She'd lived all over the country, so why come back to Whiskey Creek? "You won't get bored here?"

She burst out laughing. "Bored? Is that even possible? There's so much gossip and drama in a place like this, I bet I won't even need to watch TV. My dad didn't leave me anything but this place, but he knew this would be all I needed. I'll have a front-row seat to life in Whiskey Creek."

There was no arguing that point. Everyone knew everyone else's business in a town like this. In the city, you could be as anonymous as you wanted to be. Maybe that's why he was always drawn to urban life. But it was never as satisfying as he thought it would be. Money and holdings didn't mean squat unless there was someone else in your life, and the women he'd had relationships with only wanted the glossy outer shell, not the down-home center. Like his mother. And women like Jules understood the small-town guy, but couldn't relate to the businessman.

Hell. He'd become convinced that a woman who could appreciate and love both sides of him didn't exist. He shook away the idea of a lonely future. "Why the café? I never would have thought about converting an old filling station to a bookstore and coffee shop."

A dreamy look came over her face. "Harper and I used to go to this coffee shop in Clement, and then we'd drive to Fort Worth to go to our favorite bookstore. We used to say that someone should combine both."

"And The Storiebook Café was born."

Her cheeks tinged red with pride. "Yep." Her gaze traveled around the room. "It's nearly perfect. Just a few more things before Harper's set," she said, turning back to him, her eyes glowing. She hesitated, then added, "Thank you for helping."

He dipped his chin in a nod, that damn guilt over deceiving her that he'd been working so hard to bury resurfacing with a vengeance. "Whiskey Creek needs a place like this."

"A place where folks can hang out and not get drunk?"

"Uh, no," he said, not missing the dig at The Speakeasy. "A bookstore. Keep people reading, you know?"

"Exactly." She tilted her head slightly, her eyebrows pulling together. "That's exactly right."

They ate in silence for a few minutes and his mind wandered. He still had a short list of things to get done—not including the upstairs—but he'd made a lot of headway. In the repairs, anyway, but not in his search. Thankfully, his worry that Storie or Harper had access to Jiggs's garden room had been for nothing. There were no doors to the outside from the old filling station. "I'll get the bookshelf finished tomorrow." Hopefully. "That one damned shelf almost seemed cemented in. After that—"

After that, what? He had to get upstairs. No stone unturned. If he didn't find the miracle infused oil stuff he'd been looking for, it would crush Jiggs, and he couldn't let that happen.

She flashed him a mischievous look, and then jumped up and headed for the tearoom. "I bet I can get that shelf out," she called over her shoulder.

"Right," he said with a scoff. "I'd like to see you try."

He left the remains of the dinner, following her. Stopping in the doorway, he took a minute to watch her. He'd spent way too much time the last few days doing that. Just stopping and staring. Thinking about her, what she'd accomplished here, how hard she was working to realize her dream and Harper's with the café.

Which made guilt flare over the fact that he'd tried to swoop in and buy the place from her dad. Where would that have left her? And double guilt that he was deceiving her. His whole reason for being here was a lie. What an asshole.

She moved like a dancer, lithe in her regular uniform of jeans and white tank top. He hadn't seen her in anything else, he realized. And he wanted to. A floral dress. A miniskirt. A bridal gown.

Shit. Where had *that* come from? He cupped one hand behind his neck. And what the hell was he doing? Ever since he was a kid, he'd been halfway gone from Whiskey Creek, one foot out the door. So why was he suddenly having thoughts about Storie in the morning? Storie in the evening? Storie all day long?

And why did Whiskey Creek suddenly seem more open to possibilities?

She circled her wrist, pointed to the shelf, and then lowered her arm. Shaking out a sore muscle maybe, but it was an odd movement. She stepped forward, gripped the shelf he'd been struggling with for the last two days, and—

No freaking way. She lifted the damn thing off like it was air.

He surged forward. "What the hell? How did you do that?"

She threw a casual look over her shoulder and shrugged, but he detected a hint of something else in her eyes. Something playfully wicked, he thought. "Guess you loosened it for me," she said.

He grimaced, his good humor zapped. "I was ready to take a jackhammer to get that off. There's no way—"

She dipped her chin, looking up at him through dark, long lashes. For a second, he'd actually thought she'd exercised some magical power over him, then snap, she'd released the spell, all to make him look like an idiot.

"Guess you didn't quite hit the right spot," she said. Her crooked smile shot him off in another direction.

His brain fogged, the double meaning of her words taking hold. She'd gone from contrite over her teasing with a damn straw to a full-out siren. If she wasn't deliberately taunting him, he'd go to church every Sunday for a year—and like it. He was willing to take a chance and call her bluff. He closed the distance between them, looking down at her through his bleary eyes. "You better be careful if you're going to play games with me."

She arched a brow at him. "I'm a Hatfield and you're a McCoy," she said. "And I don't play games with people I don't trust."

She was direct, he had to give her that. "Why don't you trust me?"

One corner of her mouth lifted in a sardonic smile. "I know you're not here out of the goodness of your heart, and I'm no fool."

No, clearly, she wasn't. "So you think I'm up to no good and you're teasing me with..." He gestured up and down her body. She didn't have to do anything to torture him. Ever since she'd come back to town—hell, ever since that night at the lake—she'd ruined him for other women. "I think you've been messing with me," he said. He didn't know how she'd locked that warped shelf into place, or how she'd released it, but right now he didn't really care. He just wanted to get back to that unfinished business they had.

Her lips shaped into a small O. "Have I?"

He moved closer, ready to take their flirtation a step further. "Oh, yeah, you have."

She rested her shoulder against the unit, looking innocent and nervous, and before she had time to know what was happening, he locked his arms on either side of her, forcing her to move until her back was against the built-ins. "And I don't like to be messed with."

Her eyes flashed. "What are you going to do about it, big guy?"

He inched in. "I have plenty of ideas. That night at the lake, remember?"

As he leaned closer, the defiance in her eyes faltered and her lips parted in surprise, but he wasn't about to let her off the hook. *She'd* come back to Whiskey Creek, looking like she did. *She'd* brought up old memories and made him have second thoughts about any plans to move to Austin or Houston or Dallas. And now she was right in front of him, an innocent lamb, and he was a wolf, ready to devour every inch of her.

"We're in a bookstore, not by the lake," she said, shooting his fantasy about her right to the surface. But Christ, she wasn't backing down or pushing him away. The look on her face almost felt like a challenge. Could they recapture the magic they'd had that night?

"You told me to take a good look that day," he murmured. "I did."

She held his gaze. Her jaw tensed and she swallowed, her tongue slipping between her lips to moisten them. Oh yeah, she was rattled, but she met his gaze and said, "Guess I probably got you through some lonely nights, then. Glad to help."

He tried to hold in his laugh, but it broke free. "And now here you are—"

"In the flesh," she said.

The weight of those words struck a nerve in his gut. She was right in front of him, and what had started as an antagonistic relationship was taking a definite turn. He dropped his lips to her neck, breathing in her light lavender scent.

She groaned softly, her skin heating under his touch, her chest rising to meet him as her breath drew in. Just the sound of her voice, low and sexy, hit him deep in the gut. His body went on alert. He shifted, allowing himself the barest pressure against her hip. The touch elicited another moan, but she gripped the shelving to keep herself upright.

Which was just what he needed to do. Stay in control. With Storie, he could lose it so easily. He still hadn't kissed her, and he knew that as soon as he dove into her, his mouth against hers, that would be it. He would come undone and might not be able to stop. An old fantasy had a way of taking on a life of its own.

He had to keep his head about him. Make it last. He stretched an arm up, holding onto one of the corbels under the built-in shelves. Something moved. No, jerked. An earthquake…but they were in Texas, not tremor territory.

He lurched, losing his balance as the shelving rocked again.

It shook, knocking against Storie's shoulder. She lost her balance and staggered sideways. He went with her, losing his own footing when their legs tangled together.

One minute they'd been standing, the next they were falling. He managed to wrap his arm around her, flipping her as they tumbled to the ground, blocking her fall and taking the brunt of the impact himself.

"Oh God." She gasped. "Are you okay?"

He lay still for a beat, the blow of his back hitting the ground knocking the wind from him. Pain radiated out from the crown of his head, embarrassment causing just as big an ache.

"Reid?"

He became aware that she was still stretched out on top of him, the length of her body pressed against his. Not quite the circumstances he'd imagined, but he smiled. His body reacted, an electric charge firing through him. So this was what it felt like to have her so close.

"I'm fine," he said, his voice thick and strained to his own ears. The truth was he was anything but fine, and any second now he was going to flip her over, and—

Control. He sucked in deep breaths to stop himself from losing it.

"Are you sure?" Her words rushed out, laden with concern.

His anguish deepened. Hell no, he wasn't sure. He was lost. Utterly and completely lost. Heat rose in him like fire burning out of control. He could feel every inch of her. Her breath against his cheek. Her forearms touching his shoulders. Her breasts pressed flat against his chest. One of her knees wedged in between his legs. Her feet entwined with his.

He couldn't think straight. Guilt knifed through him over his deception, but greater than that was his desire to have his mouth against hers, his hands exploring every inch of her body. Right now, tonight, he was going to experience the fantasy that had haunted him for so long.

CHAPTER 8

STORIE COULDN'T MOVE. She *should*, but she couldn't. Reid's hands tightened on her hips, pulling her firmly against him. Was this part of his game? Whatever he wanted, he didn't have it yet, so now he was being Mr. Charming. Only he was no prince. He was a strategist. And an ordinary human. All the more reason she couldn't trust him. Of course, he'd grabbed her, flipped her, and buffered the fall. Protected her. But still...

Her mind felt vaguely fuzzy. Had her powers gone rogue, causing the shelf to shake and tossing her to the ground? The drained feeling she got whenever she tried to do a spell or purposely directed her magic was becoming stronger. As if all her energy was zapped clean out of her body and she needed a minute to recharge.

She started to roll off of him. Flirting was one thing—and she'd definitely taken it too far—but actually crossing that line with him? Bad idea. Gunpowder and lit match. He'd made it perfectly clear that he wasn't staying in Whiskey Creek and there was no way in hell she was opening herself up for a broken heart.

In the back of her mind, she heard the low noises of a machine, but she was locked in place by Reid's hands, immobilized by the explosive heat of their bodies against each other.

"What was that?" She searched for the ground to push herself up.

"Don't move," he growled. His grip on her tightened, holding her against him. "Don't. Move."

She stilled. Breathed in. Sweet Jesus, he smelled good. Smoky wood mixed with the evergreen scent of the forest. Her heart thundered. Why couldn't he have been a wizard? Maybe then she would have let herself have a little fun with him.

But he wasn't, and she couldn't. She was a witch, and no mortal man could accept that.

She had to divert his attention. Her attention. She glommed onto the first thing she could think to lighten the sexual energy sizzling between them. Behind her, the machine-like sound grew louder. "What happened with the shelf?" she asked.

His eyes darkened as he looked at her. "Good question."

"We should...check." She struggled to keep the muscles in her arms strong so she could keep holding herself up. Or she could give in to the temptation and get a taste of what she could never actually have.

Just one taste...

She dropped an inch, her face moving closer to his, their lips almost touching. Her pulse skittered and she turned her head at the last second, her cheek against his. The movement pressed their hips closer together, but she pulled away.

"Christ." The frustration behind his words danced over her skin.

"You're leaving," she said, "and I'm a-a—"

She couldn't tell him what she was. *I'm a witch*, she'd say, and he'd throw her off him, bolt out of there so fast, and she'd never see him again. She shook her head against the crook of his neck.

He moved his hands to her shoulders and pushed her up until their gazes met. His eyes narrowed. "You're a what?"

"Nothing," she said, a wall going up around her. He might want to get closure on their unfinished business, as he kept saying, but he was not her friend. Not anything remotely close to it, in fact. "I'm just...uh...wondering about that sound." The low rumble and steady sound of liquid was not like anything she'd ever heard before.

"I don't hear anything," he said, his hands moving back to her hips.

Her stomach fluttered, heat surging through her. He was making this so difficult. "I do." She pushed with her arms, levering herself up, but the way he was pinned under her meant moving against him.

A quiet groan slipped from his lips. "You're killing me, darlin'," he ground out.

She stilled, their bodies molded together. "Letting go might help."

He cracked a tense smile. "It might." But he didn't release his hold on her.

She would miss that smile. And having him around every day once the grand opening was over. And when he left town. No. She shoved the thoughts away. He couldn't be trusted, she reminded herself.

Oh boy. She planked her body and angled her hips up. "You've been really helpful with all the repairs," she said, "but I—"

He let her go, the spots where his hands had been suddenly cold. Good God, if this was her reaction to his hands on her, buffered by a layer of denim, what would it do to her to have skin against skin?

"It's been a pleasure," he said, but from the sound of his voice, she got that he meant more than the work he'd done around the shop.

She extricated herself completely, grabbing hold of his outstretched hand to pull him up to standing. He turned to the bookshelf. The loose corbel came off in his hand. A loud scraping followed and the built-in unit creaked to life, swinging open.

She jumped back. "What's that?"

Reid grabbed hold of the edge of the door, his face turning pale. "Looks like a…a secret door."

She rolled her eyes at him. "Ya think?"

He frowned. "Yeah, I think."

A rumbling, clearly audible now that it was no longer muffled by the wood shelving, came from inside. Reid started. "Stay here," he ordered. "I'll check it out."

She scoffed. "No way. My hidden passageway. I'm going, too." She put her hand on his shoulder as she crept after him, her heart in her throat.

The threshold opened to an outdoor room. She gazed up at the open sky. A secret room. Amazing. This was the stuff of books and fairy tales.

But in front of her, Reid pulled up short. He let out a string of curses under his breath, his feet suddenly rooted to the ground.

"What's wrong?" she asked, moving to his side. And then she saw it. A big contraption right in front of her. If there'd been a little girl, a key, and a boy in a wheelchair, she might have thought she'd been transported smack into the middle of the *Secret Garden* book. Instead, she looked at a fifty-five gallon wooden mash barrel and a cylinder made of riveted and soldered copper sheets, half-hidden by the trees and brush, but very much there. Several smaller glass containers were stacked along the garden wall.

"It's a turnip still," he said, answering the question she'd been thinking but hadn't asked.

"O-*kay*." She stared at the contraption. "As in moonshine?"

He nodded, his frown spreading to his eyes. "As in moonshine."

She walked past him, toward a brick wall covered in thick vines, and then inched closer to the rattling still. "Which is illegal, right?"

He made a noise in his throat. "Oh yeah."

She pointed at it, looking over her shoulder at him. "And it's...*working?*"

He walked along the perimeter of the garden room, his hand skimming over the brick walls. "So it would seem."

"And out there, beyond the wall, is that Whiskey Creek?"

"Guess you know why it's called that," he said with a laugh. "And over the wall this way is The Speakeasy."

Which, she realized, was not a surprise to him. "This is *your* still? You're a moonshiner?" She heard the shrill rise in her voice, but couldn't control it any more than she could control the flame circling in her gut, swirling like a tornado as it gained momentum. Emotions out of control meant magic out of control. Fury consumed her, and before too long, her magic would go haywire and who knew what would happen?

"Not exactly," he said grimly. "Little Joe Woodson and Gus Malone made their white lightnin' here."

She balled her fists to keep from spewing her own form of lightning from her fingertips. "And who are they?"

"Gus Malone was my great-granddaddy. Little Joe was his...business partner."

She pieced together what she knew, which granted, wasn't a lot. Kathy Newcastle had said some spirit company wanted to buy a moonshine recipe. Jiggs Malone wanted to buy this place. To expand his illegal business, or to keep it a secret?

The truth dawned on her and she faced Reid, pure fury lacing her voice and thick in her throat. "So this is why you got Buddy to leave the job. You wanted to take over so you could make sure we didn't find the hidden door."

He threaded his fingers together behind his neck, pacing, but remained silent.

She blew past him, back out to the tearoom. "Isn't it?" she demanded, whirling around again to face him. He'd used her, just as she'd known he would. He was not to be trusted, and she'd been a fool to fall for his charm. "Isn't it?"

Slowly, he nodded. "Storie, I'm sorry. I—"

At least he didn't flash her some flirtatious smile in hopes that she might brush off how illegal and unethical and…how plain horrible he was to almost seduce her, all to keep her from finding this room. "Sorry for lying? Or for getting caught?"

"Storie—"

She flung up her hand. "What am I supposed to do? Turn you and Jiggs in to the police? Become an accomplice?" Her voice raised an octave. "How could you hide this from me?"

But she didn't give him a chance to actually respond. Didn't want to hear more lies. She turned on her heels and bounded upstairs, knowing full well that she was a fool for thinking she could trust a mortal man, let alone Reid Malone.

* * *

Storie pulled open the secret door and ushered Harper into the room. "Moonshine? Are you sure?" Harper stared at the still, then at her.

"Oh yeah," Storie answered. "Dead sure."

"I never thought I'd see one of these," Harper said after Storie showed her the turnip still. "White lightnin'. 'Splo. Sugar whiskey. Moonshine." She paused for dramatic effect, looking just like Piper and Scarlett when they were giving their mama attitude. The two women stared at the contraption in silence for a good while. Finally, Harper said, "Looks to me like Gus and Little Joe were the 'shiners, but who were the bootleggers?"

Storie stared at her. Stared at the turnip still, so named because of its odd shape, then at the brick wall dividing her property with The Speakeasy. And she added it all together. "Old Jiggs Malone changed the name of the saloon to The Speakeasy back when I was a senior in high school, right?"

"Don't know. I didn't know you then," Harper said.

"Well, he did. Coincidence?"

Harper shook her blond head, her layers of hair falling perfectly back into place. "No, no coincidence."

"I don't think so, either. Kathy said that saloon's been in the Malone family forever. Goes back four generations, at least, far as I remember. And it's situated right next to our moonshine operation—"

Harper bristled. "It's not *our* moonshine operation—"

But Storie continued. She'd been working the details of how things must have been a few generations back. "So the Malones had to have been the bootleggers. And Jiggs probably changed the name of the saloon as a nod to his family's part in bucking Prohibition."

Harper tapped her fingers against her cheek. "And you think Little Joe and Gus brewed their white lightning then sold it at The Speakeasy, which really was am old speakeasy? They were the moonshiners *and* the bootleggers?"

Harper nodded. "That's exactly what I think."

But that didn't answer all her questions. "Reid probably makes a fortune with his mineral holdings, right?"

"A fortune and a half, at least."

"So why would he risk that so his dad can moonshine?" It didn't make sense, but Storie had worked too hard to open this place, and she wasn't about to let the man next door deceive her and rip apart her dreams, one bottle of moonshine at a time.

No, she was pulling the plug.

* * *

"I knew there was a way in from that side of the moonshine room."

Reid stared at his dad. "You said it was a little operation, Pop. That turnip still is hardly small. How could you not tell me?"

"You were busy running the bar. Figured it was better that you not know all the details. Just made sure there wasn't a way into our bar from the other side. Guess that didn't work out since there is a way in."

Reid growled, barely containing his anger. It was one thing to know his dad was brewing whiskey, but quite another to see the scale of the operation.

Behind the bar, Jiggs doubled over, coughing and hacking. After a good twenty seconds, his system calmed and he straightened back up. "Son," he said, "this was a speakeasy. Plenty to hide during Prohibition. The card room used to be closed off, don't you remember?"

Reid masked his concern over his father's failing health. He knew there wasn't an endless amount of time left, which was why he'd looked the other way about the moonshining in the first place. His dad wanted to leave a legacy with Gemstone Spirits. Who was he to stop that from happening?

He looked over his father's shoulder at the room behind the bar. He remembered tearing down the walls and helping to frame a new door, but he'd been a kid. He had no recollection of what the room had been before they'd gotten their hands on it.

"You should have told me, is all."

Jiggs shuffled out from behind the bar, facing Reid. "So you could stop me? Hell no. I want my grandkids to remember their pappy and to have something concrete. Apple Pie Moonshine, courtesy of Jiggs Malone. That's what your young'uns are gonna remember 'bout me."

Grandkids? Good God, maybe the old man was losing touch quicker than Reid had realized. He wasn't anywhere near having kids. He shook away the image of Storie. "They'll remember you in an orange jumpsuit, if we're not careful. Come to think of it, there won't be any kids if I'm in the cell next to yours."

"Gemstone Spirits don't care it's bootlegged liquor. They want to buy the recipe for my white lightnin' 'cause they tried it. Came by here more than a year ago, back when Teddy still had some of that damn oil of whatever it is, and they tasted the Apple Pie Moonshine. They never forgot how good it is."

Reid stared at him, his jaw slack. He'd risked everything trying to help his father, and all he'd gotten in return were lies. Just like the lies he'd told Storie. "You're kidding. She's not going to let me back in there."

That realization seized his gut.

"Son, I never kid about whiskey. Gemstone Spirits wants to taste the 'splo before they fork over the money, or the deal's goin' south. You gotta convince her to let you back in so you can finish searchin'."

Reid propped his elbows on the table, rubbing his forehead. Unbelievable. How had he ever agreed to be part of this mess? "You have to promise," he said after he calmed down.

"You can't run that still anymore. I don't want either of us going to jail, Pop."

Jiggs crossed his heart and held up two fingers. "Scout's honor."

Reid grimaced. "Great. Except you were never a Boy Scout."

The wrinkles in Jiggs's face multiplied as he cracked a smile. "Our little secret."

He added it to the long list, belonging to both Jiggs and him.

He had no idea how long he had before Storie called someone in to clear it out of the garden room, but afterward the deal with Gemstone would definitely be dead and that would absolutely kill Jiggs.

His dad's eyes, a network of thin red veins snaking through them, were wide with anticipation.

"I've looked everywhere," he finally told his father. "It's all normal stuff in the kitchen. No magical elixir. Whatever Ted Bell gave you, I think it's all gone."

Jiggs swung his cane out from under him, jabbing it point blank at Reid. "You're a Malone, son, and that means you ain't no quitter. It's there, somewhere. I feel it in my bones, and you gotta find it."

His head ached. Christ almighty, give him strength. "No, I'm not a quitter, Pop, but I know when something's hopeless. Storie isn't hiding some secret ingredient. All her dad left her was that old gas station. It's been torn apart. There's no hidden anything, besides your moonshine room."

"What about upstairs? You said you ain't been up there yet." Jiggs plopped onto a hard backed chair, stretching his bad leg out in front of him. "You said that was off-limits. That's probably where she's hidin' it."

"Maybe," he said reluctantly. He'd given plenty of thought to what he'd find upstairs, but the mystery ingredient that was worth a multibillion-dollar price tag to Gemstone Spirits wasn't the thing that kept him awake at night.

He lay there for hours conjuring up how beautiful and mysterious she was, and about what he wanted to do with her.

"Time's runnin' out, son. Gemstone Spirits'll walk away with their offer if I can't get the moonshine right."

"They're buying the recipe for an illegal whiskey, Pop. You really think you can trust them, anyway?"

Jiggs scoffed, propping his cane back on the ground and levering himself to standing. "Your mama said I'd never amount to nothin', and aside from you, son, so far she's been right. I need me that deal. I need to know I did somethin' worthwhile with my life."

Illegal moonshining wasn't the answer, at least not in Reid's book. It was understood, if not spoken, that while he was proud of Reid, Jiggs needed more than a successful son. He needed his own legacy to pass down, even if it was as a moonshiner. Reid knew he couldn't turn his back on his father. Not now. No matter how his dad had used him to get what he needed, or how many lies he'd told along the way, Reid had to do what he could to help his dad feel proud. He walked beside him, ushering him out the door so he could drive him home. "I know, Pop," Reid said. "I know."

CHAPTER 9

Storie waved her hand at the rows of upside-down flowers hanging in the stairwell. One by one they floated down, righting themselves into a five-gallon bucket. That little effort wiped her out. Her magic mojo was fading. Before long, she wouldn't have any witchcraft left in her.

Outside the door, Reid's hammer pounded against the bookcase. Damn Harper for letting him back in. But once he was here, Storie had asked him to secure the secret door until she could get someone in to clean out the room. She and Harper could expand the business and hold little girls' birthday parties there, and it could be a magical haven for Piper and Scarlett. Closing up the hidden passageway in the meantime was the very least Reid Malone could do.

In truth, she planned to take care of cleaning out the garden room. They'd leave it locked up for now, and when everyone had pushed it to the backs of their minds, she'd cast a spell and make it all disappear. If she had any magic left in her.

Her eyelids drooped, her head foggy.

As she gathered the last of the dried flowers, a dark

feeling of foreboding draped over her. It filled her lungs, snaking through her veins like oil spreading over water.

She opened the door, setting the bucket of astrids off to the side, looking around the tearoom. Nothing was out of place and everything seemed just as it should.

Harper was in the kitchen, as usual, the girls were off with their dad, and besides Reid, the shop was empty. She tried to shake the feeling that something wasn't right, but it grew.

She snuck a glance at Reid. Maybe he wasn't what he seemed to be. Where there were witches, there had to be evil, didn't there? That was one of the things her father had warned her about. "I discovered that not everything is as it seems when there's magic involved. It changes people," he'd said. "I didn't want it to change you."

Not for the first time, she wondered again if Reid could know the truth about her powers.

She considered him. He always looked like his mind was working, and now was no exception. He had his hands tucked in the pockets of his jeans, and his broad chest filled out his plain T-shirt, his biceps firm and defined under the sleeves. That tattoo peeked out from under the left sleeve. She wondered what it was, but finding out wasn't in her plans.

"Woolgathering, darlin'?"

"What?"

"You're staring at me like…like you want to devour me," he said.

Bringing on the charm full force. That's what she got for daydreaming. Before she could answer, darkness swept through the room again, washing over her like a shroud. "Do you feel that?" she asked, looking this way and that.

He cocked an eyebrow. "Feel what?"

How could she explain without sounding like a lunatic? "Like a…a dark cloud's hovering."

"It's the humidity," he said. "This is Texas."

The air did feel thick and heavy and filled with moisture, but that wasn't what she meant. "No, that's not it," she said, but she didn't have an explanation so her mind wandered again.

Straight to how it had felt when they'd fallen, how his body, rock-hard beneath hers, had sent her nerve endings firing. She redirected her thoughts. How many women did he barter with, trading labor for favors? She was probably one in a long line, all the more reason to stifle her attraction for him.

Then again, he'd been searching for the opening to the garden room, so maybe not too many after all.

The sound of the front bell dinging drew her attention away from him, clearing her head.

A woman's voice trilled, "Hello?"

Harper would answer.

"Hello?" the woman called again.

"Headphones," Reid said.

"Right." Harper almost always had her earbuds in and her iPod cranked.

The woman called again. "Storie Rae Bell?"

She cringed at hearing her full name, but Reid grinned. The smile reached his eyes and lifted his cheeks in a way that relaxed the hard lines of his face, his smile softening the bad-boy look his soul patch gave him. "Storie Rae." He muttered her name as if he were feeling the sounds of the letters on his lips and tongue. "Fits you. All Southern and mysterious."

Her name had always been another thing to make her stand out. Boys had laughed and girls had been brutal. She tried to gauge whether he was mocking her, but his gaze had dropped and now it slipped over her. He definitely wasn't laughing.

"In the back," she called out as Reid dragged his smoldering eyes back up to her face.

Oh yeah, he knew how the game was played. Just one more reason to steel her emotions and keep him at a distance. "I'm not mysterious at all," she said. Total lie, but she thought she sounded convincing.

His smile faded as he cocked an eyebrow at her, but said, "I disagree, darlin'."

For a moment, the darkness that had tinged the edges of her consciousness turned to a cold chill that started in her toes and slithered up her body. She sensed a distinct burning inside of him, like lust and desire tumbling together, fanning a hot flame. Her father had said no man could accept a witch, but was he right?

Another breeze, colder this time, swept through the room. The light, steady tread of footsteps followed. A pleasant-looking woman with ginger-colored hair cut in a stylish bob stood in the frame of the door between the tearoom and the front of the store. She wore a cream beret, a matching shawl, and underneath it, purple pants tucked into black boots.

Peculiar outfit, given that it was August.

"Can I help you?" Storie asked. The cool air vanished and the foreboding grew as the words left her mouth.

"I certainly hope so." She didn't quite have an accent, but there was something unusual about her voice. An affectation of some sort. She definitely wasn't from the South. "You're Storie Rae." Not a question, a statement.

Reid had grown still behind her, but Miranda the cat had appeared, winding herself between the woman's legs as if she were taking stock.

The woman sidestepped until the cat left and returned to Storie. "Ye-*es*," she said.

The woman clapped her hands together, but it made no sound. She rushed forward, clutching Storie's shoulders and pulling her in for a hug. Oddly, she was stiff and there was no joy in the movement.

"My name is Millicent," she said swiftly, as if she didn't want to linger on the letters and leave it hanging in the air for very long. "It's been twenty-eight years."

"What's been twenty-eight years?" she asked, forcing the words out. She glanced at Reid, but he couldn't offer her any comfort.

"Twenty-eight years since I've seen you," the woman said.

Storie's hands turned clammy. The woman's words were sluggish in her mind. Surely this wasn't… It couldn't be…

"Storie Rae," the woman said, "it's true."

"What…what's true?" she whispered, barely able to find her voice.

"I'm sure I'm the last person you thought you'd see, but I'm here now."

Her vision blurred. From shock, or maybe from tears welling in them. She couldn't be sure which. "Who are you?" she asked, but inside she knew. This woman with hair that matched her own, eyes that sparkled with flecks of gold, and with the odd aura shimmering like a cobalt blue band outlining her body. There was only one person she could be.

"I'm your mother," the woman said. Her thin voice sent a chill down Storie's spine.

"My mother."

"You can call me Millie."

Millicent. The room spun. God, how could this be happening? She needed to sit down. To put her head between her knees. To stop shaking.

Millie continued, completely oblivious to the emotions coursing through Storie. "I was very sorry to hear about your father passing. I'm sure he did his best raising you. You look like you turned out satisfactorily, but I imagine you have some questions, yes? There were certain things, of course, that he couldn't teach you. Are you quite all right? A bit tired, perhaps?"

Every tied-up emotion Storie had felt from the moment she learned her mother had chosen to give her up came spinning out. "You let him take me," she said, her voice trembling and hollow. She couldn't keep up with the direction of Millie's sentences. She didn't care what her father had or hadn't been able to teach her. What she cared about was that her mother hadn't wanted her.

"Water under the bridge. Ted's gone now, so the pact I had with him is null and void."

Storie's blood chilled in her veins. She had an urge to run. To get far away from here, but she couldn't. Of course she couldn't. Harper was counting on her. Piper and Scarlett needed their happy ending.

She looked to Reid again, searching for a lifeline. An invisible thread connected them for a quick moment. Right this second, it didn't matter *why* he was at the café, or what ulterior motive he had. Even the brief conversations they'd had suddenly held more weight than anything her mother could possibly say.

He came up next to her, his shoulder brushing against hers, bolstering her with his mere presence. His body emitted heat that took the edge off the chill encircling her, and when he placed his hand on her lower back, his strength seeped into her, giving her enough gumption to swallow her nerves and realize what Millie had just said. She stilled her racing heart, steadied her breath, and asked with an unbelievably calm voice, "What pact?"

Before she answered, Millicent waved her arms and

uttered something Storie didn't understand, and Reid froze, turning to a statue before her eyes.

"What did you do?" Storie yelled. She wrapped her wrist around his and felt his pulse under her fingers, but he didn't stir.

"He'll be fine," Millicent said, waving away her concern. "Your father didn't know there were three of you. True, it was a horrible miscarriage that I never told him, but it was better that way. Astrid and Declan stayed with me, and your father took you. I gave him the seeds to the flowers. I knew you'd be able to grow them. I could keep track of you through them. Every time you grew them, it was a conduit to you."

Her mind reeled, taking everything in. "Declan and Astrid?"

She nodded. "You have a brother and sister."

Triplets. Her head still swam from that bomb.

"You don't fit in here, Storie Rae. You're a witch, and you belong with me. With Declan and Astrid. I never should have listened to your father, but we can fix things now. We need you."

Astrid. The name of the flower seed her father had given her. She racked her brain, trying to remember the story, but her mother seemed to read her mind.

Her head felt heavy and her heart stopped beating for a moment. "The flowers were…are like a touchstone?"

"If you will."

She bit her lower lip, her eyes burning. "You kept the other two, but gave me up? Why?"

Millie shrugged. "I could have kept any of you. I cast a spell to decide. You floated up out of your bassinet."

Floated up in her bassinet? She couldn't even fathom that. "Why'd you come back?" she asked. She'd grown up without her mother, and it was too late to fix that. Things were going well. She had The Storiebook Café. She had Harper and the girls. Even Reid seemed to be here for her. But her mother? She suddenly felt as if she were in a snow globe that was being shaken.

"You're one of three, an anomaly. Connected in a way that doesn't often happen in the magic realm. They need you now. You must return to unite the trinity." She continued before Storie could ask any questions. "They're not complete without you, just as you aren't whole without them. You feel your magic waning, don't you?"

The dizziness. The weak knees. Her witchcraft really was fading?

"They need you. Get your affairs in order here, close up your quaint little shop, and you can return with me. I'll take you back to where you belong."

Her limbs felt heavy, rooted to the ground. "I don't understand," she finally managed to say. "You want me to leave Whiskey Creek?"

She glanced at Reid. He was frozen, his arm in the air, the hammer gripped in his hand, the gray-blue of his eyes unmoving. His body was encased in gossamer webbing.

He'd commented that she had no friends. Maybe this woman—her mother—was right. She pressed her hands against the sides of her head, confusion clouding her thoughts.

"You should know from experience how difficult it is to live in one world when you belong in another. If you cross the gap to the magical realm, through the seam, you'll be able to do everything you're not able to do here. You'll be united with your siblings. Your power will grow and multiply." She glanced at Reid then, and added, "And you'll be safe."

A chill ran up her spine. Was she in danger? Was that why her father had always kept them on the run?

The woman nodded, as if agreeing with Storie's thoughts.

"No fear of discovery. No fear of persecution. No worry that people will judge you and won't show up to your little opening. The whispering and the curious stares will all stop. You'll be free."

She started, taking a step back. She and Harper worried that the opening would be a bust, that they'd end up staring at each other. "How did you…"

"I know everything about you, Storie. I know that Harper is your closest friend. Your *only* friend. I know that your father put his head in the sand about your powers, but you can't pretend away who you are, and you can't deny that you feel incomplete. I know that your favorite place is the fishing shack at the lake, and I know that summoning thunder and lightning makes you feel in control. But just wait. When you're reunited with your brother and sister, then you'll know *real* magic."

"But how…?"

Millicent glanced at the bucket of dried flowers. "They kept us connected. I may not have been here by your side, Storie," she said, her gaze flashing to Reid's immobile body for a split second, "but I've been here."

An ominous blanket pressed down on her as she processed what that meant. Her mother had known about her all these years, but had never come forward.

"Yes, I've known."

"Why now?"

"Because it is time. I was powerless before, but now the pact is broken. Your siblings need you, before you all wither away. Because you must be together to survive."

Storie sank to the ground, trying to wrap her head around what her mother was saying. Just when things were starting to come together for her. Just when she'd finally begun to figure out how to balance who she was with the life she wanted. Just as she was finally putting down her roots. Why now?

The woman gave another long, pointed look at Reid again. "You're a *witch*, Storie. No one here can know who you are. *What* you are. Your father knew. Surely he made you see that. What I did with your father was a mistake, and it cost me you. Mortals can't accept you. They don't understand magic. They can't, and you must protect yourself. But you must decide before it is too late, and if you refuse, the deaths of your brother and sister, and your own eventual demise… they'll all be on your head."

Her head throbbed, her breath short. "Do I have a choice?"

"You always have a choice, my dear. The question is whether you make the selfish choice or the right one."

She exhaled, defeated. Was leaving Whiskey Creek the right choice? She didn't know, but she listened to her mother tell her about Declan's and Astrid's fading power, about their weakening spells, and she realized that she couldn't be the one responsible for their deaths. If she had the power to help then, she had to take it.

"Okay," she said.

A satisfied smile played on Millie's lips. "The right choice," she said. "You will cross beyond the seam with me when the moon is full."

Miranda meowed, rubbing up against Storie's leg. Storie looked at Reid again, feeling his vacant gaze on her even through the strands of silken thread. She didn't even know if she liked him, but she was drawn to him. Unfinished business. And when she left, they'd never have a chance to finish it. The knowledge made her heart clench.

"He wants something from you," the woman said, "but it's not what you think."

Storie's attention flew back to him.

Millicent—her *mother*—continued. "People share only what they want you to know, nothing more, nothing less."

She fiddled with her hair to hide the blush she felt creeping to her cheeks. "I have a pretty good idea what he wants."

Her mother narrowed her eyes, looking at him, then at her. "Do you?"

And then, *poof!*, she melted into thin air, leaving Storie to pick up the pieces of the life her mother had just torn apart.

* * *

"Reid? Are you okay?"

Storie's voice sounded far away. She leaned over him, her lips thin, her eyes wide. He'd collapsed to the ground and now she crouched next to him, her hands on his shoulders. Christ, what had just happened? He shook his head, trying to clear the cobwebs. The last thing he remembered, the strange woman had appeared, claimed to be Storie's mother, and…and that was it. Everything after that, until this moment, was a blank.

He brought his forearm to his head, closing his eyes for a second. "What the hell was that?"

"I-I don't know. You fell."

He peered at her. "I fell?"

Her face turned ashen, but she nodded. "Yes, you fell."

Right. And he had some prime property in West Texas selling for a cool ten million. "What time is it?"

She moved one hand from his shoulder. Checking her watch, he guessed, but he didn't open his eyes to confirm.

"Eight twenty-five," she said.

He remembered checking his watch as he and Storie had been interrupted by the woman. That had been at around eight o'clock, so he'd lost about fifteen minutes.

Where had they gone? "What the hell happened?" he asked again.

She sat back as he propped himself up on his arms. "I already told you. You fell."

"Bullshit." His vision finally cleared and he looked more closely at her. Her face was still pale and her lips had turned blue. "What happened?" he asked for the third time and with slow deliberation. "Was that really your mother?"

She hesitated for a minute before saying softly, "That's what she said."

"Do you believe her?"

Her hands clenched. Above them, the ceiling fan began to spin, gently at first, then with more power. "I don't know."

He came to a sitting position, and then stood, grabbing the hammer. "I think you have a few secrets, don't you, Storiebook?"

She scoffed, the color returning to her cheeks. "I guess you'd know, wouldn't you?"

He responded with his own question. "Your name might lead people to believe you're an open book, but you're not, are you, darlin'?"

She opened her mouth to speak, but seemed to think better of it, instead turning on her heel and stalking off.

As he watched her disappear into the kitchen, all he could think was that she was anything *but* an open book, and every minute he spent with her, he became more and more curious about what, exactly, she was hiding.

CHAPTER 10

From the minute Reid stepped into The Storiebook Café to the moment he left, he had one eye searching for some clue about the special moonshine ingredient, and the other eye watching Storie's every move. He couldn't figure out what it was about her that puzzled him. And set him on edge. And made her more interesting than any other woman he'd ever met.

The thing was, he knew she was just as intrigued about him. It had been pretty damn obvious from the other night, and that was both a huge turn-on and a huge stumbling block. He didn't want ties to Whiskey Creek, and Storie was here to stay. But damn it, he hadn't been kidding when he'd told her they could have some fun together. At this point, it felt like they had nothing to lose.

Reality smacked him upside the head. He was here for one thing, and one thing only: to find the missing ingredient for Jiggs's moonshine. If it were here, he'd find it.

He'd searched high and low, checking everywhere he could think of, and still nothing. No more secret rooms, hollows in the wall, or hidden cubbies.

Storie and Harper kept busy all day, every day, often staying until Harper's little girls were dead tired. Tonight was no exception. They'd all spent the day stocking books, coffees, and teas, finalizing the grand opening menu, and doing a million other last-minute details. The scent of cinnamon from Harper's baking floated in the air.

Piper and Scarlett stood in the doorway watching Reid put the finishing coat of paint on the wainscoting around the garden room. They chattered nonstop, making him laugh and throw his hands up in mock exasperation when they begged to help him.

Storie passed through the garden room, stopping as the girls asked him for the umpteenth time if they could help him paint. She put her hands on her hips and scolded them, looking damn sexy in her jeans and red, bleach-spattered top. He smiled to himself. She wasn't afraid to get her hands dirty, that was for sure.

"Girls, you need to leave Mr. Malone be. He's got things to do."

She didn't look at him. Interesting. In fact, she hardly spoke to him. Ever since that night when her mother had shown up and he'd lost those precious fifteen minutes, she'd stayed as far away from him as possible. She'd gone about her business at the shop on autopilot, focused on getting everything on her precious lists done, but the smiles he'd seen when she and Harper had first taken ownership and during the majority of the renovations were gone. She'd lost the joy she'd had about opening the shop, and for the life of him, he couldn't figure out what had changed. A veil of sadness seemed to have draped over her that she couldn't escape.

"We just want to help," Piper whined.

Scarlett lifted her chin, her lower lip plumping in a perfect little pout. "Why can't we paint?"

"Because we're running out of time," Storie said. "Assuming anyone even comes," she muttered.

He frowned. He'd rally the townsfolk and make sure the opening was well-attended. "We'll do a mural," he told the girls. "In the tearoom." The second the words left his mouth, he wished he could pull them back. The Gemstone people would be here any day and he still didn't have the ingredient for the moonshine. The renovations were nearly done and The Storiebook Café would be open and he'd be shit out of luck. The clock really was ticking, and the only way to keep looking was to get closer to Storie, a complication neither one of them seemed to want.

"Piper! Scarlett!" Harper called from the kitchen, her voice getting louder as she passed through the tearoom and into the former garage. "Having a party without me?"

"Not likely, Harper," Storie said. "You *are* the party."

"Don't know about that, but I am the food," she said with a tired smile. "Two more days and the grand opening will be over, thank goodness. Then we can get on to our regular business. I need routine."

"Me, too," Storie said softly, but the smile he expected to see didn't appear. No encouragement for Harper. No pep talk about the end being in sight.

Harper looked at her, concern etched in the tired lines on her face. "You okay, sugar?"

She waved off the question. "Fine. Just beat."

Oh no, it was way more than that, he'd bet that secret moonshine ingredient on it. He sensed the tension emanating from her. She wouldn't look him in the eye. Would hardly look at Harper. He knew she didn't want him here, but she'd also given up fighting him about it. Whatever was bugging her had taken hold like a virus and was spreading.

"It's late," Harper said. "Time to call it a night. Have a

drink and go to bed." She gathered up Piper and Scarlett, and ushered them toward the front. "Let's get a move on."

Storie walked out with them. If only he could help her somehow, but there wasn't anything he could do. If his mother suddenly appeared after years of silence, he'd definitely be freaked, no question.

He packed up his tools for the night, shaking his head. He was busting his ass to get this place in shape for their grand opening, and she acted like he wasn't even here, barely acknowledging him when she walked by. Which pissed him off more than it rightfully should. He didn't want encumbrances. Didn't want to get involved with her at all. But all that fell out the window as Harper's voice faded away and Storie mounted the stairs to her loft.

He could call it a night like they had and go home, but his renovated Victorian off the square was big and empty and he didn't particularly want to go to his empty bed and his incessant thoughts of her.

He could go back to The Speakeasy. Jules would be there, and all he'd have to do was crook his finger and she'd come home with him.

But he didn't want Jules.

Damn it, he wanted to experience the fantasy he'd been having for the last eight years, the one they'd come so close to living out the other night before they'd stumbled into the moonshine room.

He wanted Storie.

He headed for the stairs, but at the last second, he detoured to the kitchen. A good bottle of pinot noir or Cab sounded good right about now. He'd put his friend, Jason Santiago, in touch with Harper, and Jason had brought over some sample bottles from his Hill Country Winery. Reid looked in the pantry and was rewarded with a bottle of Shiraz. He grabbed it, found two glasses in one of the cupboards, and opened the wine. Cupping the glasses in his palm, he took the stairs two at a time.

A peace offering, and maybe a fresh start between them.

***

Storie turned on the faucet, filling the old claw bathtub with hot water. She looked around the bathroom for a bottle of bath milk or salts or bubble bath. Anything to help her sink into a blissful oblivion, even for just a few minutes.

Nothing.

She was about to utter a spell but she spotted the bucket of dried astrids she'd brought upstairs. Perfect. She pulled out a stem and ran her hand over them, siding the rough buds free. Opening her hand over the tub, she released the blossoms, allowing them to float down. They spread onto the water, releasing their sweet, intoxicating aroma. The scent reminded her of the brisk cold of an autumn day. Soothing and invigorating at the same time.

She couldn't get her conversation with Millie off her mind, and she still didn't know what to do. Give up her life here, help the family she didn't know, and not be forced to hide who she really was, or…stay here, keep hiding, and suffer the consequences. Her mother hadn't laid it out, but the message had been clear. If she didn't give up Whiskey Creek and The Storiebook Café, she'd be sorry. The veiled threat had been weighing her down ever since. She knew what she needed to do—hell, she'd agreed to it—she just didn't want to.

The flowers tinted the water a faint blue. Tiny flecks of glitter swirled and intermingled with the blossoms. She slipped out of her jeans and tank top and dipped a toe in.

Tepid, but with a spell it was heated to the perfect

temperature. Even that made her tired, but maybe it was just her imagination playing tricks on her.

Or maybe it wasn't. Everything her mother had said repeated in a loop in her head. Her brother's and sister's magic was fading, and hers would, too.

Her fingers tingled from the effort of heating the water. Her powers had always made her an outcast, but she couldn't imagine her life without them. They were part of her. If she wanted to keep her magic she really didn't have a choice. She'd have to go through with leaving to save them all.

She stepped in and sank into the tub, sliding down until she was completely submerged, fighting the tears burning her eyelids.

The hot water and the scent from the flowers didn't clear her head. Leaving Whiskey Creek, Harper and the girls, and The Storiebook Café... The truth all circled in her mind. Reid's face came to the forefront. She'd been watching him for the past week as he worked through every item on her list, the memory of his hand on her back, his smile, and his voice commingling in her mind.

Watching him when he didn't know she was looking, her breath stalled the two times she'd seen him pull his shirt off, revealing his muscular chest, broad shoulders, and strong arms. And that tattoo. His jeans hung low on his hips, revealing the waistband of his boxers underneath. Once, he'd turned to face her. She'd ducked out of sight and had to utter a spell to mask the stuttered breath that came after she managed to suck in a lungful of oxygen. His stomach had that six-pack rippled effect and a spattering of dark hair that trailed to a thin line, snaking beneath his jeans.

A flutter circled low in her stomach, moving lower until she ached inside. Ached for Reid and his touch.

Music. She needed music to get him off her mind. She couldn't afford to spend time thinking about him, not when she had two days to get everything in order with The Storiebook Café so Harper, Piper, and Scarlett wouldn't have to worry about anything and their dreams would come true.

Not everybody's could.

She snapped her fingers and Bach filled the air. Even that small effort made her sleepy. Closing her eyes, she sank deeper into the water, making a mental list of all the reasons to steer clear of Reid Malone. Much more fun to think of that than to dwell on the responsibility she had to siblings she'd only just learned about from a mother she didn't even know.

CHAPTER 11

REID HAD A RECURRING FANTASY. It always started with Storie calling his name in her throaty voice, just deep enough to be tempting and still plenty feminine with just a hint of Southern accent making her sound sweet. What a blessedly intoxicating mixture *that* was. In his head, the pickup truck from that summer night had been replaced by her Jeep, but she was soaked through, her wet tank top clinging to her body, taunting him. "I want you, Reid," she'd say, and then a soft, satisfied moan would escape and she'd whisper, in his ear, "I've always wanted you."

He shook his head, erasing the image from his mind. He rapped his knuckles on the door upstairs, but the strains of Bach filtered through. The volume rose, then dipped. Interesting. Given the name of her cat, he'd pegged her for a Miranda Lambert kind of girl. Pistol Annies and maybe even Taylor Swift, but not one of the masters. She was full of surprises, and he was curious about each and every one.

He knocked again. The door was cracked open. He pushed through, almost calling out her name, but holding his tongue at the last second.

She was no damsel in distress. He didn't know what she was, but he wanted nothing more than to find out.

The room was empty. Okay, not empty of boxes and furniture, but empty of her.

He took a moment to note the details of the loft. The kitchenette and bedroom shared the space, with what he assumed was the bathroom through a broken door, half hanging off its hinges, in the back. The music originated from there. Boxes were stacked against one wall. The floor was torn up and the kitchen looked like a tornado had touched down.

His eyes zipped to the queen-size bed pushed into the corner. *The fun we could have there*, he thought, but a sound in the back caught his attention. Maybe the bottle of wine would be enough to seduce her into that bed with him, but he didn't want to think too much about that yet. One step at a time.

God, how could she stand to live in this place? Come tomorrow, he'd move his tools up here and at least make it livable for her. Crafting a mental shopping list, he walked toward the bathroom, pouring wine into the glasses as he moved.

Behind the door, the water ran. He ran his hand over his face. Storie in the shower. Christ.

At the crooked door, he raised his hand to knock on the frame and caught sight of her reflection in the mirror. And just about lost every last trace of oxygen in his body. She lay in crystal blue water in an old-fashioned claw-foot bathtub, her arms cradling the sides, her head reclined, eyes closed.

He should turn away, shouldn't spy on her like this, but he couldn't move. Could hardly breath. There was something about her and water. His body instantly reacted. He was mesmerized, drawn to her as sure as a damn bee was drawn to pollen, and his blood pulsed with desire.

He took his time looking at her, memorizing every last detail. Her hair was wet and floated in the water. Her face held a peaceful expression and her lips curved up, the barest hint of a smile on her lips.

After a moment, she raised one arm in a gentle movement that reminded him of a ballerina.

And then the music changed. Grew softer.

His spine stiffened. She didn't have a remote. Red flags shot up in his mind and his thoughts circled around until he settled on a few of the stories he'd heard back when she'd been a senior at Whiskey CreekHigh School. *She's a freak. A demon. No, a witch.*

He'd dismissed them as fairy tales. Witches weren't real, and yet... Something about the way she moved her arm struck him.

But the thought catapulted away the next second as she stretched one leg out onto the edge of the tub. Her hands slipped beneath the water, and her back arched just enough that the curves of her breasts broke the surface of the water. His breath roared in his lungs and all he could think about was how he wanted to sink into the water with her. He wanted to make a little magic of his own with her.

Distracted, he loosened his hold on the glasses in his hand. They clinked together, and her eyes popped open, her head whipping around.

"Didn't mean to startle you," he said calmly. More in control than he felt. He pushed the door open all the way as her startled gaze met his.

Her arm flew out of the water, her fingers pointed at him as if she could unleash a beam of lightning and strike him dead, but she breathed, drew her hand into a fist, and sank beneath the water. "What are you doing here? I told you, upstairs is off-limits."

Trying to figure out how to have you, just for a night. "You've

STORIEBOOK CHARM

been stressed. Thought a little wine might help." He held up the glasses and the bottle of Shiraz.

"I'm taking a bath," she said, a husky layer to her voice.

"So I noticed." He cracked a suggestive grin. "Got room for me?"

Bold, he knew, but why the hell not just ask for what he wanted? A week ago they hadn't seen each other in nearly a decade. A few days ago they'd been at odds. But now, why not enjoy each other's company for a night?

She balked. "Are you insane?"

Very well could be. Getting close to her was the last thing he should let happen, and he suspected that once he did have a taste, he'd be addicted. And addiction didn't bode well for someone ready to leave town. It just meant he'd be back for more and never truly free.

But, he reasoned, he had nothing to lose. He hadn't found what Jiggs needed, and pretty soon he'd have no reason to be at The Storiebook Café, which meant he wouldn't have many more chances to make this offer. And if he stuck to his plan, Whiskey Creek would be a speck in his rearview mirror before too long.

"Quite possibly," he said. He approached the tub, doing a double take. Bubbles. There hadn't been any a few seconds ago, but now a thin layer skimmed the surface of the water.

He blinked. What the...?

Working here, then tending to the bar and handling his business holding, must be getting to him. His imagination was working overtime. He held the glass out to her, but she didn't reach for it. "You have a lot of nerve barging in here, Reid Malone," she said, fire lacing her words. Or maybe it was desire. "I told you, I don't need you up here."

He smiled. "You sure about that?"

She stared at him, her eyelids heavy. "I'm sure. I've avoided you—"

"Ever since your mother showed up. I know. But before that..." He left the sentence hanging. He'd felt her gaze linger on him while he worked. Let her imagine the hard lines of his body under hers.

Her tongue slipped out from between her lips. "Before that..." She swallowed.

"There's something between us, Storie. You can't deny it."

She ran her hand over her wet hair, gathering it into a bunch between her fingers. "There's not—"

"There is." He continued without giving her a chance to respond. "I think you've been thinking about me just like I've been thinking about you—"

"I think you're thinking way too much," she interrupted, but her gaze met his and a thread of understanding passed between them. She felt the connection, too.

She fluttered her hand under the water, the bubbles in the tub growing. A nervous action, he realized.

"Are those magic bubbles?" he asked, laughing. "Making you deny what you're feeling?" The thin layer of bubbles had foamed into airy white fluff, covering her chastely. More chastely than he liked, but he knew what was underneath it all.

"Yeah, something like that."

He shrugged. "You can't get anywhere in life unless you take the bull by the horns. I'll wait for you out here, if you'd prefer."

"I'd prefer it if you'd go home."

He held up the wineglasses again. "And let a good bottle of red go to waste? No can do, darlin'."

"Is that what you do? Take the bull by the horns, knocking down everything in your path? Reid, this isn't a good idea."

He clenched his muscles against the physical ache he felt for her. Covered with bubbles or not, she was his fantasy come to life. He gave her a half-cocked grin. "That's right. Knock-down, drag-out, hands on, full frontal assault. Whatever it takes. And it most definitely *is* a good idea."

She stammered over her words, finally saying, "I'd like to finish my bath."

He grinned. "No problem. See you when you're done."

He kept his eyes glued to her as he slowly backed out of the bathroom. She moved her arm, under the water, and then she smirked as the broken door to the bathroom slammed shut.

How the hell had she done that? Maybe he'd imagined it being broken. Maybe the bubbles and his ache for her had clouded his mind.

The minutes crept by. He sipped his glass of wine while he waited, taking the opportunity to scour the loft for any possible hiding places. He didn't hold out much hope that there'd be hidden nooks up here, but he'd pretty much exhausted everything else he could think of, and he was out of options.

With one ear listening for the creak of the bathroom door, he searched. He started in the kitchen, peering under the sink and into each cabinet. He examined the walls in the combined living space/bedroom, but the solid brick facings were intact, without so much as a crack in the mortar. Unusual given how old the building was. He ran his hands over the brick interior wall behind the boxes, searching what he could see of the floor for a loose board or removable grate.

He groaned. Nothing.

The floor was last, but with all the boxes piled up, he couldn't get a good view of the whole thing. Still, nothing raised suspicion.

"Find what you're looking for?"

He cursed under his breath. So much for his alarm—he

hadn't heard the door creak. "Caught me, darlin'." He held his hands in the air like the bandit she thought he was.

He turned to face her. He'd half-expected her to shut down his fantasy by bundling up in sweats and a fuzzy robe, but the Texas heat worked in his favor. She'd put on sleep shorts and a matching spaghetti-strap top with some sort of white cotton trim. Little yellow flowers decorated the fabric, and only the slightest curve of cleavage plumped from the V-neck of the bodice. But it didn't matter what she wore. She could be layered to kingdom come, and he'd still think she was the most interesting, alluring woman in Texas. Hell, anywhere.

He watched her, mesmerized by the sway of her body as she moved, almost imperceptibly. Enraptured by every inch of her. She wasn't one of those women who flaunted her beauty or figure, but she emitted more sex appeal wearing conservative pajamas like her little floral set than if she'd been in some sort of saucy stripper get-up.

Although he wouldn't turn away if she *were* in a sheer black teddy edged in red satin.

He moved toward her, more slowly than necessary, trying to keep his focus on her eyes instead of the indignant pucker of her pink lips.

Not that focusing on her eyes did anything to deflate his attraction. The gold flecks in them were like magnets, drawing him in, holding him captive. He swallowed the desire rising in him, gathering his control before he said, "Love what you've done with the place."

She clutched a towel in one hand as she angled her head, looking like she was ready to fire off a retort. Her hair was nearly dry, he noticed, but he hadn't heard the hair dryer. Another benefit of the heat, he guessed.

Her gaze settled on the bottle of wine and glass he'd set

on the nightstand. She made a beeline for it, knocking back a healthy swig. "I've been a little busy downstairs," she said.

The glass was half-drained, he noticed. Not good. Yes, he wanted her mood to soften, but he didn't want to ply her with alcohol and have her regret anything later. A one-night stand was only fun if both parties were on board with it and had no expectations.

"And it's looking great down there. Almost ready."

She brought the glass to her lips and took another sip, slower this time. Her tongue slipped out, curving up and over her top lip, holding the position for a few seconds. He wondered what it would feel like to be on the receiving end of that tongue, to feel the warmth of it against his mouth, meeting his. He'd had the briefest taste and it had left him aching for more.

"Yes," she said, breaking the spell. "Thanks, again."

She turned and set her wineglass on the nightstand, bending over to towel-dry the last bit of moisture from her hair. His pulse ratcheted up. He dragged in a ragged breath, working hard to steady his urge to ravish her right here, right now.

She flipped her hair back, meeting his gaze, smiling sweetly. "You can go now, Reid."

Oh, but he couldn't. Those lips, and those eyes. Even her voice drew him in. She couldn't possibly know what she was doing to him.

Or did she?

CHAPTER 12

Oh boy. She was playing with fire. Her mother had made it clear. People were not always what they seemed, and she'd implied Storie didn't know what Reid wanted. From the hungry look in his eyes, it seemed absolutely clear. An undeniably sexual energy sizzled between them. She was trying hard to ignore it, but how much longer could she hold off?

Then again, he'd come up here while she was in the bathtub, bringing her wine to...to...what? Loosen her up so he could get her into bed? That seemed to be one of the things he was after. No mystery there.

She ought to be appalled, but instead, she was more drawn to him. He'd been right when he said she'd fantasized about him since that day at the lake. She had, over and over and over again.

She downed half her glass of wine before setting it down and running the towel over her already dry hair, more as a distraction than anything else.

He looked good. Enticing. Ravenous.

"What are those dresses for?" he asked, pointing to the two outfits she'd been considering for the grand opening.

She dragged her gaze from him to the dresses, trying not to think about how her skin heated when he looked at her. She could sense his desire, as if he wore it like an aura.

She tossed her towel on the bed frame and picked up the first dress, holding the dark pink, black, and yellow silk in front of her, letting it hang to show how the whole thing was split up the center and how the hem angled down in the front.

Since he was here, she might as well get his opinion. She'd made her decision—get through the grand opening, make sure everything was in order for Harper, then leave with her mother. If her siblings needed her, she had a duty to go to their aid. But she couldn't let on to Harper that she was leaving. She couldn't muster a good-bye, and so the party would go on and she'd pretend that all was well.

"This is option one," she said.

He didn't say anything for a minute, and then nodded, just once. "Nice."

Okay. So maybe that one wasn't the best. She tossed it on the bed and snatched the other one, holding it up. It was a teal-colored floor-length maxi dress with a halter top.

"Eh," he said, unimpressed. "Hard to say unless I see you in them. Try them on."

Right. Like that was going to happen. "Never mind." She grabbed the scarf dress off the bed and hung them both back on a portable rack she used to hold her clothes. "I'll just wait for Harper."

"Seriously. Try them on. I'll be more honest than a woman will," he said. "Harper won't want to hurt your feelings."

"And you certainly don't care about *that*," she said, only mildly miffed. She actually liked the idea of a man being honest and telling her what he thought, and part of her wanted to just have her moment with Reid. Her whole life was changing, and she was losing everything she'd worked so hard for. She knew there was no future for them—a witch and a mortal man—but...

He didn't answer, instead moving next to her and pulling the two dresses off the rack, holding them out to her. "Try them on."

His voice seeped under her skin and took hold, as if he'd exercised some magic spell on her instead of the other way around. Her brain stuttered, not sure what to do. Making him exit the bathroom had been hard enough, given that he'd wanted to stay rooted to the spot. She couldn't make him go against his will, and she wasn't sure she wanted him to. Their hot and cold flirtation had solidly embedded him in her mind. She could go a bit further and model for him.

Why not? "Okay," she said, taking the hangers from him.

"Great." He flashed her another one of his cocky half-grins. "Then we can make a list. Pros and cons for each dress."

She stared at him, her jaw slack. "Are you mocking my list-making?"

He feigned innocence as he glanced at the rack. "Not at all. I think your lists are helpful. I can think of all kinds of things we could make lists about. *Why you should let me up here to work. Why we should finish this bottle of wine. Why you should let me into your bed.*"

Her breath stalled at his last sentence. She'd thought it, but hearing him say it sent her heart into a frenzy. "What?"

He'd zeroed in on a sheer lacy number with a creamy underlining from her rack of clothes. He grabbed it and handed it to her, taking back the other two. "And *why you should wear* this *to the opening.*"

She arched one eyebrow. "*That* dress?"

"It's perfect."

She swallowed, met his gaze, and stumbled back. He

burned with a sexual energy so strong it almost knocked her down, the heat emanating from him palpable. This thing between them, this thing she'd been trying so hard to avoid… maybe she couldn't. Maybe she *shouldn't*. She had two nights and then she was giving up her business, her dream of settling down in Whiskey Creek, and her life. Would it be so wrong to give in to the desire she felt for Reid Malone?

"No," she choked out. "I mean, yes." She didn't do one-night stands, and she wasn't about to start now. "No sharing my bed," she managed.

"And this dress?" he said, holding up the sheer number. "It's yours, so why the hell not?"

"Because," she said, "I've never even tried it on. It was one of those impulsive buys that made sense at the time."

He held it out to her. "And it still makes sense. This is the one. Try it on."

She was tempted. She couldn't give in to the other request, but this was tame enough, and she *was* curious to see how it would look. Or maybe she was just curious to see his reaction to seeing her in it. "Okay," she finally agreed, a deep-seated yearning coiling inside her.

He smiled as if he'd won a battle in a waging war. Which he had. She'd caved and was going to give him a private viewing of one of the sexiest dresses she owned.

She took it from him, turned on her heel, and hurried off to the bathroom before she changed her mind.

She had her PJs off and was just getting ready to slip the lace cami dress over her head when a quick rap came on the door. "These, too."

She hid behind the door, cracking it open just enough to see what it was he wanted to add to her outfit.

He glanced over her shoulder, his jaw tightening, as he handed her a pair of short brown-and-pink cowboy boots studded with pewter beads.

She took them, but frowned. "Boots and this lacy number?"

There was a heavy pause and his voice was raspy as he said, "Just try them."

Without another word, she closed the door. She was very definitely playing with fire.

* * *

He leaned against the wooden frame of the bed and waited, trying to block the image of her he'd seen in the mirror, but her naked backside was seared into his memory.

"You're crazy, you know that?" she called out a second later.

He summoned up his control. "Like a fox."

"I can't wear these boots with this dress."

"You can pull it off." He knew she could, and he couldn't wait to see her in them.

Nothing *but* boots would be a good look, too, but he'd save *that* image for later.

A minute passed, but finally she opened the door and stepped out. The light from the fixture behind her created rays of light that fanned out and made a soft glow around her. His breath caught in his lungs for a second as he looked at her. The top layer of the dress was sheer cream-colored lace and completely transparent. The layer beneath, with the light shining through, was the same tone as her skin and sheer enough that he could see the V rising between her legs and the outline of her waist. The fabric hugged her shape, accentuating every curve. Both layers hit her a few inches above the knee. Oh God, he was in trouble. With the boots, she looked like a freaking angel sent down from heaven just for him.

All his desire for her took hold. "That looks damn good," he said thickly, the lust balled up in his throat.

"Yeah?" She didn't seem to pick up on the strain in his voice. Moving to the full-length mirror propped up at the far end of the bed, she looked at herself head-on, turning to the side, then to the back and peering over her shoulder. "I, uh, need a slip."

Facing front again, her cheeks had blushed. She had her arms crossed in front of her, and she kicked one leg out. "The boots actually work, though," she said, sounding amazed.

The whole thing worked. He hadn't been planning on making a move, not really, but now he couldn't stop himself. He reached her in two strides, coming up behind her and looking at her in the mirror, the heat from his eyes burning as he admired her.

She met his gaze in the reflection, but didn't speak. It was as if she knew what he was going to do before he did it, as if he were under a spell that he didn't want to break.

He moved a little closer, closing the gap between them until her back was pressed up against him. Her lips parted and her eyes closed. Then, as if she made a split-second decision to go with the impulse of the moment, she opened her eyes, lifted her arms, laced her fingers behind his neck, and leaned back against him. "We shouldn't do this," she whispered.

"But it'll be fun." His hands skimmed her sides, snaking around her waist. His fingers spread on her stomach, moving over the flat surface and something hard. A belly button ring. Christ. He ached to touch her skin underneath.

He dipped his head, pressing his lips against her neck, never taking his eyes off her. Her breath caught as he slowly spread his fingers. His head swam, weighed down with the fog of desire coursing through him, but he didn't want to scare her. Baby steps.

This was what she wanted, he could feel it in his bones, but he held back. Patience. The word kept circling in his mind. They couldn't start something tonight and not finish it, and he wanted to make this last. Make her want him as much as he wanted her.

He was going to give her just enough to make her want more. Beg for more. Fun and merriment. That's what he'd called it, but really it was a far more serious game they were playing.

He watched her in the mirror as he caressed her breasts with one of his hands, slowly sliding the other down across her belly again, fingers spread. She arched her back against him. She was his. "No regrets," she muttered, her half-mast eyes meeting his in their reflection.

"No regrets," he agreed. He held her gaze as his hands dropped to her sides, the fabric of the dress layers bunching in his grip. He played with the hems until he pulled them both up, exposing the flesh above her knees. Higher, exposing her thighs.

"No regrets," she said again, this time barely audible.

Higher, revealing a glimpse of the white thong in the mirror.

Her breath ragged, she gasped as he touched her. So gentle, but the heat from her burned against his skin. She moaned, deep and low and sultry, and that was it. He was gone. She was dragging him down to the depths of his deepest desire, finally fulfilling the need simmering inside him for too long.

Irresistible. He couldn't wait any longer. His lips found her neck again, his eyes still glued to her reflection. She broke the connection, turning her head up to him until her lips brushed his. He'd dreamed of this moment. Spent far too many years settling for substitutes while he longed for Storie. And now here she was, finally.

He pulled back. Pushed her dress up, running his hand across the soft flesh of her stomach, his gaze hitching on the silver swirl at her navel before sliding up to her breasts. He kept his other hand busy, lightly teasing her. A slow torturous burn until she came undone.

He kissed her neck, nudging her face forward until he held her aroused gaze in the mirror again. Her body called for his touch. His mouth. His tongue. His full attention.

Patience.

His own breathing grew shallow. As much as he wanted her this second, he resisted. Barely.

She raked her hand through his hair and arched against him, her back pressed to him, her eyes fluttering closed. She tried to turn her body toward him, but he stopped her, holding her firm.

"Not yet," he said. She could make all the lists she wanted and think she was in charge, but right now, he wanted her to let go. But damn it if she didn't try to take control. She moved against him, grabbing his head and trying to turn again.

A veil of fog slipped over him, but he managed to say, "Not yet," and this time, he held her by pressing his hand against her lower abdomen. Christ, he didn't know how long he could resist having all of her. If she tried to turn around again, he'd let her, and then he'd throw her on the bed and take her, body and soul.

With half-mast eyes, he slid his gaze up her reflection, slowly and deliberately. This was a moment with Storie he never thought would happen. His eyes traveled across her browned stomach, her supple breasts, nipples half-exposed. Christ almighty, she moved her hips, the pressure against him driving him wild.

Patience, he told himself for the third time. Aloud he managed to growl, "Stop."

She opened her eyes, the heat in them scorching him.

He dropped his hands, breaking the connection. "I told you we could have some fun," he said, grinning. Truthfully, raising one corner of his mouth was all he could muster.

She leaned back against him again, her breath labored. "This isn't fun," she said, her voice barely above a whisper.

"Of course it is." He had to touch her again. He wanted to hear her moan. To say his name. He met her bleary gaze. "We can't close the gap on eight years so fast."

She straightened and tried to turn around again. She wanted to move past the slow burn he was raising in her, and he tried to resist, but he simply couldn't. This time he was going to let her.

"Reid."

The voice was far away, coming to him through a fog of desire.

"Reid."

Oh God. The person calling him wasn't Storie.

A woman's voice called him again, his name drifting up the stairs. Goddammit. Jules.

Storie pulled away, her gaze still locked with his in the mirror.

Quick footsteps thundered in his ears as someone mounted the stairs. He stepped back and his head dropped. Lacing his fingers behind his neck, he muttered a string of curses under his breath. By the time he looked up, Storie had yanked her dress down to cover her body again. Jules stood at the doorway.

"There you are," she said, waltzing in as if she'd been in Storie's loft a million times.

Storie started to speak, but Reid moved toward Jules. "What the hell are you doing here?" he ground out, barely controlling his frustration.

"Looking for you, of course." Jules dragged in a deep

breath, tilting her head back and looking around. "God, it smells good in here. Like cinnamon and fall."

Storie's hands twisted in front of her. She hesitated, her lips pursed, but she finally pointed to the bucket of dried flowers. "They're astrids. Very fragrant."

"Nice." Jules turned back to him. "Your dad's been looking for you—"

As if something suddenly dawned on her, she stopped, looking from him to Storie, and back. Her expression changed, her lips pulling into a pronounced frown, her brows knitting together, and her hands opened and closed nervously. She knew exactly what had just gone on between them. Or what had almost gone on.

Reid's spine stiffened, his heart stopping for a beat. "Is he all right?

"Yeah. Sure. He thought you'd be back at the bar by now, is all. I said I'd come on over and find you."

He breathed out, relieved.

She scanned the room, her gaze hitching on the discarded dresses on the bed before she turned her attention to Storie. Flipping back a loose strand of her bottle-blond hair, Jules gave Storie a good once-over. "Are you Harper or Storie?" she asked through a tight smile.

"Storie Bell. Harper's gone home for the night with her daughters. This is my *apartment* you're in," she said, her voice terse.

"Huh." Jules seemed oblivious to the anger emanating from Storie, but Reid felt it circulate in the air like a dark cloud. "That's a killer dress," she said, looking her up and down. "Isn't that a killer dress, Reid? Not sure about the boots, though."

"It's a killer dress," he said. He only wished he could get Storie all the way out of that dress. They'd been so close.

But thanks to Jules, that wasn't going to happen right

now. He took her by the arm and headed for the door, but she slipped out of his grip and turned back around.

"Reid sure does love a girl in boots," she said, trailing her own booted foot in a half-circle on the floor.

Storie's eyes narrowed. "Is that right?"

Jules touched his hand again, grinning up at him before turning a hundred-watt smile at Storie. "Sure is. He's a cowboy, after all. A wanderer. His mind's always on some dusty road to somewhere else. He's only here till he can find more of what your dad gave Jiggs to make his whiskey so tasty."

"Jules," he said sharply. Christ. What the hell was she doing?

Storie looked up sharply. Her eyes narrowed. "What?"

He flashed a death look at Jules, then turned it inward on himself for continuing the deception with Storie. It was his fault for lying, but now there was no way to come clean. She wouldn't believe him either way. "She doesn't know what she's talking about."

Jules's lips formed an innocent circle. "You didn't tell her what you've been looking for?"

"No." Storie's cheeks tinged red, the blotchy color spreading to her chest. "No, he neglected to mention that."

"That's enough, Jules," he ground out. He took her arm and directed her to the door. "I'll be back over to the bar in a minute."

"Sure thing." She raked her eyes over Storie again, a smug, satisfied expression on her face. "Great to meet you, Storie."

"Enlightening to meet you, too."

Once they were alone, he turned to face her. Damn Jules. Damn Jiggs for chewing the fat with her about the moonshine. And damn himself for not being straight with Storie in the first place.

"Jules was out of line," he said. "Storie, I—"

"Stop." Storie's face tensed and she squared her shoulders. "She just told the truth."

"I didn't mean to—"

"To what, Reid? Didn't mean to manipulate your way in here so you could search for something belonging to my father? Didn't mean to get caught? Didn't mean to try to seduce me so you'd have access upstairs? All of the above?"

He closed the gap between them. "Didn't mean to hurt you."

"I'd have to care to be hurt," she said coolly, "and I don't." She walked past him, stopping at the doorway, holding it open, and waving him through. "Thanks for stopping by."

He stared. "Straight denial, then? What, we can't talk about this? Yes, your father gave Jiggs something that he put in his damn moonshine, and now it's gone and I came here to see if I could find more—"

Her eyes turned cold. "That's what you've been after this whole time?"

Crap. Scarlett's question about whether he was a prince or a bandit came back to him. There was no way for him to come out of this looking like anything but a bandit.

Her hands fisted, her wrists circling. The moonlight shining in from the windows faded, the sky outside darkening. A crack of thunder broke the silence of the night, a streak of lightning following.

"So that turnip still? That thing in the secret room behind the shelves downstairs… That thing isn't just an old relic? It actually belongs to your dad and *he uses it* and you really *have* been helping him?"

He started to move toward her, but she held up her hand. Heavy pressure against his chest stopped him, as if she held an invisible weight up to him. "Darlin', you're blowing this way out of proportion."

"I should have known." She shook her head, turned on her

heel, then whipped back around to face him. "My mother warned me. She was right."

This was a losing battle. He shoved his hands in his pockets, trying to stay calm. "She warned you about what?"

"That you wanted something, and that I better be careful."

"First Kathy Newcastle, now your mother. They're both right, Storie," he said. "I started out looking for something, but you've been in my head for years and I want you, not some magical ingredient for my dad's moonshine."

"I'm not that girl anymore—"

"No, you're not—"

"So that fantasy of yours can just shrivel up and die," she said, making a small movement with her hand.

He stepped backward toward the door, his feet moving without him thinking about it. What the hell was happening? How had everything gone to shit so quickly?

"Storie," he said, the pressure against his chest closing in on him until he felt like he would explode. "You have this all wrong."

She moved toward him, and for a second he thought maybe he'd gotten through to her. Her face softened, but she gave him a sad smile. "It doesn't matter," she said, grabbing hold of the door. "My mother was right. I don't belong here anyway."

What the hell did that mean? But before he could say another word, she closed the door.

CHAPTER 13

THE FIRST DAY of the rest of her life, that's what today was. She'd tossed and turned the night before, her encounter with Reid making her alternately cringe with embarrassment and ache for him. The whole thing had shaken Storie to the core. She was not the kind of woman to have a one-night stand with a man she hardly knew. And she'd come so close to crossing that line. How, when she knew he'd been using her all along? God, she was a fool.

Her skin pricked, a rush of cold dancing over it. He'd been upstairs, not to see *her*, but to search the apartment. She'd stepped out of the bathroom to find him moving boxes and poking at the floorboards. And she'd ignored the rush of suspicion she'd had, burying it when he'd looked at her with unabashed desire.

She'd taken him at face value, believing that he was just filling in for Buddy Garland, but he had to have paid Buddy off to get him to leave the job and insinuate himself in the role.

And, oh God, she'd let him *watch* her in the mirror as he'd nearly brought her to climax! Hell, she'd tried to *help* him. Thank God Jules had shown up when she did.

What was wrong with her? "What's it mean?" she asked, her voice soft and sleepy.

She shuddered, trying to push it all aside and focus instead on what she needed to do to finish getting the shop in order. Outside the front door, the little stray terrier cried. She grabbed a bowl from the kitchen, tore up some chicken Harper had left in the fridge, and set it outside for the dog. The flowers she'd conjured were wilting in the summer heat. Raising her hand, she started to give a quick flit of her wrist, but stopped. She needed all her energy today, and that meant no magic, even if the grand opening suffered for it. It was too draining.

No. It was just her imagination. Her mother was lying, just as Reid had been, but the dizziness and fatigue after she used her powers kept growing. Millicent had said her brother and sister were losing their powers and she felt hers slipping away, too. She was losing everything, and she couldn't do anything to stop it.

The dog barked her thanks, lapping up the treat. She bent down and scratched her head. "I guess you can stay," she said. "Harper'll need a good watchdog."

She barked again, and it almost looked like she was shaking her head. Gloom surrounded Storie. The feeling was becoming too familiar, and she didn't know if it was her doubt creeping in over the idea that she was leaving, Reid's betrayal, or something else entirely.

The dog finished eating and looked up at her sweetly, the expression on her face reminding Storie of Blake Shelton's smiles. That's what she'd call her. "Shelton. Goes with Miranda, the kitty, so I guess that'll work, even if you are a girl and Blake and Miranda aren't together anymore."

Shelton yapped again. Good, she liked the name. Storie

went back to the kitchen and added dog food to the grocery list.

A minute later the bell at the front door dinged. Surely Shelton couldn't...

No. She peered through the serving window between the kitchen and the shop. Millicent.

She had a tendency to just appear, which rattled Storie. Was this what it was like in the magical world—wherever *that* was? Witches and wizards just showed up, unannounced, whenever and wherever they wanted to? She'd have to get used to that.

A few seconds later, she appeared in the kitchen. "You're having second thoughts," Millie said.

"They'll pass."

But Millie didn't look so sure. Her brow furrowed. "What's going on?"

The silver lining to what had happened with Reid was that she was wary. Yes, this was her mother, but Storie wasn't ready to reveal her every thought. "Nothing," she said, offering a circumspect smile. "I thought I was going to settle here. I didn't expect to leave so soon."

"Things don't always work out how you plan them. Declan and Astrid need you."

"Their powers?"

"Fading fast," Millie said. "As are yours."

The flowers. She looked at the back of her hands, flipping them to study her palms. Maybe it wasn't that she was distracted and sad at leaving Whiskey Creek. Maybe it was that she was being drained of her magic because she needed her siblings as much as they needed her.

"Declan and Astrid." She let the names roll off her tongue. Her brother and sister. They sounded foreign. Unnatural. Not like Harper, Scarlett, and Piper. And Reid.

"Well, Millie—er, Mother," she said, wishing she could

stall for more time, but at the same time feeling as if she needed to cut her losses. "I'll be ready after the grand opening."

Her mother's eyes, a mixture of onyx and cobalt, swirled, the colors mixing like the waters of a churning ocean. "Eleven o'clock at the lake. We'll go when the moon is full."

One more day hardly seemed like enough time to get everything in order and say good-bye to her life, but she'd made her choice. Last night with Reid, she'd felt a glimmer of hope that maybe he *was* her Prince Charming, and that The Storiebook Café really *did* hold the key to her happily ever after. He'd made her feel like no man had ever done, and for a blessed chunk of time, she let go and gave in to the pleasure.

But it had been an illusion. There was no Prince Charming or happily ever after. Life, after all, was not a storybook.

"Eleven o'clock," she said. "I'll be there."

CHAPTER 14

STORIE MET Harper at the curb an hour later, and handed her the revised grocery list. Piper and Scarlett popped out of the car. "I'll be back in an hour," Harper called through the open window.

Storie followed Piper and Scarlett inside—and nearly ran them over. They'd spent a few days with their dad, and now they stood with their feet rooted to the ground, taking in the transformed café.

"Guess you found your everlovin' mind!" Scarlett exclaimed, a dramatic hand over her heart. Scarlett O'Hara had nothing on Harper's little girl. Storie felt sorry for the men she'd eventually manipulate with her theatrics, but as long as she kept her gumption and her confidence, like her namesake, Storie knew she'd be happy. "It's like a fairy-tale shop smack in the middle of Texas!"

Scarlett unstuck her feet and raced to the crazy-quilt patterned overstuffed love seat and flopped onto it, her white eyelet-edged denim skirt settling around her little legs until just her red boots showed. "It's lov-ally," she said, shifting from being a six-year-old Katie Scarlett to being a cockney-accented Eliza Doolittle.

Storie caught Reid's eye through the pass-through window between the book room and the kitchen. What was he doing here?

He'd shown up the day before and she'd steered clear of him, letting Harper handle the last of the repairs. She knew he was still looking for some magical thing her dad had supplied to Jiggs, and she didn't care. She had too much to do to get things in order for Harper.

She did not want to face him. Did not want to remind him of what they'd done in front of the mirror, and did not want to remind herself of how he'd used her.

But seeing him now, her blood boiled. He had some nerve.

With the girls here, though, she was forced to focus on them. "It *is* lovely," she said, heat from being in the same room with Reid overwhelming her. Feeling his gaze on her had almost the same effect as the touch of his hands, as much as she fought it.

He sidled out from the kitchen and sat down next to Scarlett, bouncing the single cushion—and Scarlett with it—from the unbalanced weight. Acting like nothing had happened between them. Anger swelled in her, but he appeared unfazed.

"What do you think, Piper?" he asked. "Do you think it's lovely, too?"

Piper's gaze darted from one area of the room to another. She studied the front counter with books displayed on shelves beneath the wood top and clusters of orchids in small terra-cotta pots. She slowly walked the perimeter of a tile cutout defining the seating area of the café, one careful step at a time. Gingerly, she trailed her fingers along row after row after row of the books Storie had sorted and organized on the floor-to-ceiling shelves. She climbed three steps of the sliding ladder, before finally turning around, her eyes glazed. "It's a fairy tale," she said, one side of her mouth lifting into a crooked smile. "Most definitely."

Tears pooled in Storie's eyes, but she felt Reid watching her and quickly blinked them away. This *would* be her legacy. She had just a few hours left to make sure it was perfect before she left this little family she'd worked so hard to create. She fought the emotions welling in her. Leaving would be the hardest thing she'd ever done.

Scarlett tugged on the hem of her shirt. "What's wrong?"

She forced a smile and ruffled Scarlett's hair. "Not a thing, sugar." She led Piper and Scarlett around, letting them examine every nook and cranny of the café. Reid brought up the rear, hovering as though he wanted to say something, but he held his tongue.

Good. She didn't want to blow up at him in front of the girls and she didn't think she'd be able to stop herself if he pushed her.

They went through the kitchen, the tearoom, and the indoor garden room, avoiding the secret moonshine room. They didn't need to know about that yet. The girls oohed and ahhed the entire time, noting every loving detail she and Harper had put into the place. They noticed the *fleur de lis* pattern stenciled on the walls—a magical touch. The heavy glass jar of Red Vines and the bright flowerpots sitting on an antique sideboard she'd found at a garage sale. The arrangements of dried astrids scattered everywhere, scenting the air with apples and cinnamon. The tray of white chocolate and cranberry scones that their mom had made, and that Storie had pulled from the freezer to try.

They even recognized the beat-up white drafting table that Harper had brought with her from her marriage and that was now in the tiny office off the kitchen. They stopped to gape at the fancy hats and boas hanging from hooks on the dress-up wall, trying each one on, throwing the lengths of feathers around their necks and twirling in front of the oval mirror.

Reid stood next to her. They watched in silence, but she absorbed his freshly-cut-grass scent, his Ropers, the plaid button-down shirt, and the cowboy hat. He'd been as cowboy as they came back when she'd first been in Whiskey Creek, and he still was.

The girls scampered into the garden room. She started to go after them, but he spoke, the sound of his voice anchoring her where she stood. "We need to talk."

She looked straight ahead, sucking in her cheeks, her jaw tight. Her fists clenched and she fought the energy pooling in her core, spreading to her limbs. No magic. Not right now. "We have nothing to talk about."

He drew in a deep breath as if he were summoning strength. "Oh yeah, we sure as hell do."

"No. We don't. You like your fun, but if you think you can waltz in here with your country-boy charm—"

"That's not what I'm doing. Yes, I was poking around upstairs while you were in the bath—"

"No, you came upstairs with wine. You *knew* what you were doing. You *used* me."

"That's how it started, Storie," he ground out, "but wanting you, and wanting to help my dad, are two different things."

That did it. She threw her hands up in the air. She wanted to strangle him, that was all there was to it. "Are they really? You didn't think you could soften me up to make your search a little easier? And there I was and you just thought, hey, since she's there and naked—"

"No, that's not what I thought, but Jesus Christ." He barely controlled the anger she could see brewing under the surface. "You've been in my head for a long time, darlin' and, yeah, I want you, and if I didn't have that country charm, I wouldn't have stopped and I sure as hell wouldn't be here right now trying to make things right."

A tangle of nerves coiled in her gut, and heat rose to her cheeks. What was she supposed to say to that? He'd touched her like no man ever had, and she'd felt things she'd never experienced before. But the blow of knowing he'd just used her, seizing the opportunity for a little fun when what he really wanted was something else entirely—well, that just proved she was a fool.

"Fun, isn't that what you said? No regrets?" Her anger with him morphed into more disappointment with herself. He'd been crystal clear about what he wanted from her. Fun and merriment. Nothing more, so why should she feel betrayed or used?

It was her own fault. He'd convinced her to try on that see-through dress without a slip and when he'd given her a good once-over, looking like he was ready to eat her alive, she'd fallen for it.

She steeled her nerve. "You were looking for something. I get it. You used me, and I let you. But we won't have to worry about that anymore after tonight."

His jaw tensed, his blue eyes clouding with iron gray. "And why is that?"

Her insides felt like they were being ripped apart. She blinked back the burning behind her eyes. "Because I'll get someone else to finish renovating upstairs and you can go back to your bar, or get the hell out of Whiskey Creek, or make moonshine, or do whatever it is you plan to do with your life."

Without another word, she left him in the tearoom as she chased down Piper and Scarlett, wanting to spend as much time with them as possible before tonight.

***

Reid watched Storie go. What else could he do? He had no choice but to wash his hands of the whole thing. He stayed put for a minute and watched her spin around the room with Scarlett, acting like he didn't even exist. Not that he could blame her. From where she sat, he had to admit that it looked bad.

He could have told her why he'd taken over the renovations for Buddy. He could have just been honest, but his experience with the truth, and women taking him at face value, never boded well for him.

Beginning and ending with his mother. He'd been nine when she'd decided to leave Whiskey Creek and Jiggs, had packed up her things, and had pulled him out of bed to go with her. "You'll live a small-town life if you stay with your father," she'd told him when he cried.

He'd wiped away his tears and asked, "What's a small-town life?"

"Living here," she'd said, "in a square town, never doing anything with your life."

He'd told her the truth—that he liked their town, and he didn't want to leave his dad, and he'd make plenty of his life. He thought it would be enough to make her stay, but she'd just dabbed at her own eyes and shook her head. "It's not what I signed up for," she said, and then she'd up and left, never looking back.

If she could see him now, she'd know that he'd done plenty. He was worth millions, even if he didn't flaunt it. Buying up property in Whiskey Creek meant he owned the gas and mineral rights to more Barnett Shale than anyone in the county, and the blessed units were far and wide. He'd done okay for a small-town boy living in a square town.

Okay, but he was still alone, and kept thinking, as his

mother had, that maybe the answers were somewhere outside of Whiskey Creek.

The bottom line was that his boneheadedness meant that Jiggs was out of luck with the moonshine deal with Gemstone Spirits. There was no magic elixir to add to the moonshine recipe. He'd blown it with Storie *and* had failed his dad.

What a banner day.

CHAPTER 15

THE LONESTAR BOYS were the best honky-tonk band in all of Somervell County. They showed up right on time and set up out in the garden room, the music filtering in through the tearoom and into the front of the shop. Wine bottles from a local winery were lined up next to sodas and water bottles, tables of appetizers scattered in every room. Harper had spent all afternoon finalizing the offerings. The aromas could be smelled three counties away, and now everything was set up and ready to go. Harper had hired a sitter for Piper and Scarlett, and Storie's heart broke when they said good night. Because she knew she was saying good-bye.

They still didn't know if folks would show up, but they'd done everything they could, and now it was out of her hands.

Reid had left by mid afternoon, sending a friend to finish everything up. Now it was time. Her heart pounded, nearly bursting out of her chest. She couldn't be sure if her anxiety stemmed from worrying if folks would show up, or over the ticking clock counting down the minutes to the end of her life as she knew it.

Both felt equally bad at the moment.

She took a last look around her loft. Everything was in place. What she wasn't taking with her, she'd boxed and had stacked against the back wall. Her mother had been right. Her magic was fading, but she mustered up enough to repair the counters in the kitchenette and to spruce up the floors. Harper would be able to rent the room out if she needed extra money. Everything was all set.

She ran her hands down her sides, ready to face the guests. To launch The Storiebook Café with Harper. And to say good riddance to Reid.

* * *

Reid tipped a bottle of beer back and took a long drink. He'd finished half the bottle waiting for Storie to walk into the front room. He almost didn't come, but he thought that seeing her one more time might get her out of his head once and for all.

His friend Jason Santiago stood next to him, a bottle of Cab in one hand, a stemless wine tumbler in the other. "Slumming it with beer tonight, eh?"

Reid took another swig, grimacing. "I'm not in the mood for complexity." Things with Storie had gotten real complex, real fast. He wanted to go back to his simple life. The bar. No encumbrances. No worries besides Jiggs.

"Just want to get drunk. Got it." Jason absently swirled his glass, releasing the aroma of the deep red liquid. He brought the glass to his nose and breathed in, then took a drink. "Best crop so far," he said proudly.

Reid frowned, remembering what the wine had done to him and Storie. "The Shiraz is pretty good, too."

"A good wine can act like a love potion," Jason said. "Or so I've been told." He winked, grinning.

A week ago, Reid would have laughed and told him to

give him a case of his best, but not now. Not unless it was Storie drinking the potion and falling, enamored, into his arms.

And that wasn't likely to happen.

So far, the grand opening had garnered a decent turnout. Clusters of men and women came in, looking at books and magazines, drinking and laughing. He looked around, satisfied. People were curious, and he was pretty sure they'd have come on their own, but he'd pulled in some favors and rallied his friends. The Storiebook Café was going to be a hit.

Next to the beverage table, Harper had arranged appetizers and sweet treats, colorful summer napkins and paper plates. A local college student perched on a stool behind the cash register, ringing up gift and book purchases as people shopped and checked out.

That little mangy terrier Storie'd taken in sat outside the front door, head tilted, looking forlorn. How a dog could be so expressive, Reid didn't have a clue, but that pup sure was. She scratched at the door, and Harper hurried over, cracked it open to let the dog in, then shooed her through to the tearoom and up the stairs.

"She's a beauty," Jason said, holding his glass up and pointing to a tawny-haired woman walking into the front room, snatching a bite-sized appetizer off the sidebar as she passed.

She wore her hair in a shaggy, layered cut that worked with the flouncy floral blouse and jean miniskirt she had on. He looked at her, long and hard. He couldn't pinpoint why, but she looked out of place. And familiar. Maybe she'd been in The Speakeasy, but, really, what did it matter? Yes, she was gorgeous, but no one compared to Storie.

The party had spilled out front with people swaying to the honky tonk under the *porte cochere*, the new sign, done up in fairy-tale writing declaring The Storiebook Café to be a *Novel Experience*, swinging in the breeze. The rain had come and gone over the last two days, the weather reports completely unable to predict when and if there would be showers at all.

Puzzling, but at least it was clear now.

Harper made the rounds, mingling, straightening products, restocking the food table, reshelving books and magazines that had been haphazardly laid down on the window seat or one of the tables.

And still no Storie.

One more beer, and then he was leaving.

Harper rushed into the kitchen carrying an empty tray. She returned a minute later, the tray loaded with some sort of steak-wrapped mushrooms, the smell of ginger and garlic swirling through the room in ribbons he could almost see. The air changed and he suddenly knew Storie was coming. He took another drink of his beer as he looked back toward the tearoom and the stairs…

And nearly choked.

The dress.

Christ almighty. She was wearing the goddamned dress… and the boots.

She didn't meet his eye, but he knew in his bones that she'd worn it just to torment him.

"So I take it that's her, then," Jason said, leaning against one of the bookshelves.

"What?"

Jason held his wineglass up, pointing toward her. "From the way you're staring, I'm guessing that's the woman who's got your balls in a vise."

He tried to drag his gaze away from Storie, but his head swam and he couldn't think straight. He grunted.

"Poor son of a bitch. You should never let a woman get

under your skin like that." Jason said something else, but all Reid's attention was on Storie.

She was an enticing combination of tasteful and utter sex appeal. The dress stopped a few inches above her knees, and she'd put on a black slip to make it more demure, but it didn't matter. She'd never looked sexier.

She'd gathered her hair up in a loose mass at the back of her head, ginger curls spiraling down and framing her face, a few strands trailing over her shoulders. Truth be told, it looked as though she'd just tumbled out of bed after having had the greatest pleasure of her life and had hurriedly thrown herself together.

She looked sexier than any woman he'd ever seen. Seeing her again did not rid his mind and senses of her. Shit no. Seeing her again branded her into them, her image, her scent, everything about her burned into his skull. He'd never escape.

He wasn't the only one who'd noticed her. Beside him, Jason was riveted, and every man in the room had his eyes on her. She was a goddess, but he'd be damned if he was going to let her see just how deeply she'd affected him. Their eyes met for a split second, and she flashed him a defiant smile, but she turned and quickly went back the way she'd come. Maybe back upstairs to hide, because she had to be as affected as he was.

From the back garden room, The Lonestar Boys launched into Luke Bryan's "Country Girl", and a high-pitched squeal made the hairs on the back of his neck stand up. He knew from experience at The Speakeasy that it was the most requested country line-dancing song. As he peered through the window of the front room and through the panoramic windows of the back room, he could see that the cleared dance floor was empty.

STORIEBOOK CHARM

Nobody jumped in to start the whole thing. Too bad. Dancing was always a good icebreaker at a party.

"You done fixing up this place?" Jason asked.

"Guess so." But if there was a chance in hell that he could get Storie back, he'd take it. Jiggs would be pissed, but Reid didn't have a choice. Storie was more important.

"Uh-huh."

He ignored Jason's skeptical tone. After tonight, Storie had said, it wouldn't matter. That one sentence had been bugging him. Was she going to ban him from coming into the café? He couldn't let that happen. He didn't think he could stand not seeing her.

They stood, people-watching for a minute, then Jason knocked him on the back of his arm. "Where'd that woman get off to?"

"The gypsy one?" Reid searched the crowd. No sign of her. He shrugged. "Sorry, dude. Lost her." He finished off his beer, tossing the bottle in the trash. "Later," he said, glancing out the window toward the garden room again before heading to the front door.

He stopped cold. Harper and Storie were in the middle of the room, leaning forward and shimmying, then rocking back, doing a right kick, and crossing their left legs over their right.

They were leading the line dance, and like a damn hypnotized boy, he walked through the tearoom, through to the back, and stopped. He watched, riveted, as she met his gaze, that defiant smile on her lips. The taunting look seemed to be her telling him that two could play this game, and her move was to make him suffer.

She was succeeding.

Everyone in the room disappeared and it felt as if she were dancing just for him. She ran her hands up the sides of her body, across her breasts, and above her head, swaying her hips, bending her legs, and turning her back to him. But she looked over her shoulder, flashing him a half-smile that said she knew exactly what she was doing, and how much it tortured him.

"That woman knows how to dance," someone said from behind him.

"Shit yeah," another guy said with a grunt, and Reid knew just what they were thinking. He fisted his hands, fighting the urge to pummel them both right here and now. He had no claim on Storie, and even if he wanted one, he'd blown it by sneaking around the café behind her back, but he sure as hell didn't want anyone else looking at her. Fantasizing about her.

He wanted this dance, this private show, just for him.

"Don't give her up, man."

He broke the invisible thread connecting him to Storie and looked at Jason. That mangy dog stood next to him, looking up at them with a pouty look on her face. "What?"

Jason smirked. "Come on, dude. I don't know what's going on with you two, but look at her." He pointed to Storie and the energy emanating from her with every move she made. Magic. "That's all for you, man."

He swallowed. Hard. Burying the desire coursing through him and shaking away the image of waking up next to her, day after day. Of seeing her smile, of hearing her laughter.

The song ended and she turned to Harper, shutting him down cold.

The singer stepped to the mic. "The next one's for all the star-crossed lovers out there." The guitar strummed and he broke into the tortured song "Tomorrow" by Chris Young. The lyrics struck Reid like an arrow to the heart. There was no way he'd ever get Storie out of his head until he'd tasted her, caressed her, touched her, and made her his, completely. There was no tomorrow.

STORIEBOOK CHARM

"Go on," Jason said, giving him a shove.

No other prompting was needed. He moved across the room, his gaze burning into her back.

She turned as he came up to her and without a word, he took her by the hand, pulled her in until her body pressed against his, and let his hand slide to her lower back, his fingers spreading as he dragged her closer.

"What are you doing?" she demanded.

"Dancing."

"I don't want to dance with you, Reid. We're done."

She could say she was done till the cows came home, but her voice cracked, just enough that he knew he'd gotten to her. He held her other hand tight, straight down, pressing their joined palms against her leg.

He dipped his head and murmured in her ear. "What did you expect me to do after that show you just put on, darlin'?"

"That wasn't for *you, darlin'*."

"Wasn't it?" he asked as the singer belted out the next lines of the song.

The music surrounded them, cradling them together until not even a breath of air hung between them. He edged his leg between hers, the heat of her against his thigh. He held her tighter, never wanting to let her go. If she resisted, he would let her go, but she didn't. Instead she bent her legs, ever so slightly, working herself closer. He moved one hand to the side of her face. With the other, he kept her firmly in place.

"I think it was all for me," he said, his lips perilously close to hers.

She'd so effectively tortured him with her dance show. Now it was his turn. He slid his fingers through her loosely knotted hair. He grabbed hold, gently, and tilted her head back, barely able to stop himself from locking his lips to hers, from devouring every inch of her. If he kissed her, there'd be no stopping. There'd be no freaking tomorrow.

He forced himself into a slow rhythm, bringing her along. They fit together, like interlocking blocks.

"I-I should check on Harper," she said, barely managing to swallow the stammer in her voice and choke the words out.

He rocked against her, shaking his head. "She's fine."

"But..."

She seemed to forget whatever she was going to say as he dragged his lips across her neck. She melted a little under the heat of his touch. If she responded like this to his lips on such a chaste part of her body, what would happen if she were bare to him? "I'm sorry," he whispered.

She nodded, barely. "It's tonight or never." She moved her hands to the sides of his face and tried to move his head so their lips would meet.

"We've got all the time in the world," he said. Granted, he felt as if he were going to burst if he couldn't have her, but he wasn't going to make it that easy for either of them. Anticipation was half the fun, and he'd waited for eight years. He was going to have her, yes, but he was going to go slow and make sure they both enjoyed every blessed minute.

"Kiss me," she said.

The words sounded like a desperate plea, but instead of complying, he let her go. "Uh-uh, darlin'." Not here. They needed privacy.

CHAPTER 16

A SHIVER WOUND through Storie when Reid released his hold. Damn him for making her feel this way, but it was her own fault. He was right. She'd danced for him. Only for him. And why the hell not? This was her last night here. For a moment, the world had melted away and it'd been just the two of them, alone. It didn't matter that he hadn't been straight with her, that she was leaving, or that there was no future in it for either of them.

He took her by the hand and pulled her into the tearoom and into the stairwell leading up to her loft. The scent of the astrids floated around them, left over from when she'd had them hanging to dry. He started upstairs, but she yanked on his hand and he jerked to a stop. She scurried up the steps past him, whipping around and putting her hands out to the sides, pressing them against the wall and blocking him.

"I can't go upstairs with you, Reid," she said, looking down at him, wishing she had more time. Eleven o'clock was going to come too quickly.

"Not even to finish that dance in private?" His hand moved slowly up the back of her thigh, brushing the edge of her dress. A rush of heat crashed through her. If he kept going, he'd reach her bare bottom, the thin strings of her thong mere scraps of lace.

Her body reacted, independent of her mind. She should push him away. Triple-check that everything was in order, go change her clothes—what did a woman wear to a cross over to a parallel magical world, anyway?—and drive to the lake. Instead, her back arched as his hand skimmed over her behind, feeling the strip of lace cutting over the pulsing center between her legs.

"N-no, I c-can't." She could scarcely get the words out. Reason battled with the blood pulsing through every inch of her.

Reid didn't know the clock was ticking and her time in Whiskey Creek was almost up. He kept his distance from her, using only his hand as he circled it back to trace the outside of her leg, his touch feathering around to behind her knee. He skimmed his hands up the sides of her body until he was tracing the neckline of her dress. "Sure you can."

"I-I can't," she said with a stammer, but she inched closer to him. The flutter had started in her stomach when she'd moved for him on the dance floor. Now she closed the gap between them.

He pulled at the neckline of her dress down. The heat of his gaze singed her skin. Footsteps in the tearoom brought her back to reality. She broke the connection, a chill winding through her. "We c-can't do this," she said, but instead of fixing her dress and leaving him alone on the stairs, she edged farther up, sinking into the shadows.

"Oh, but we can." He prowled up the steps after her, catching her and pressing his hands against the walls, his mouth the only contact between them.

"Reid—" she whispered. She wanted him to devour her. God, why didn't he touch her? Her head swam. All she wanted was his hands roaming her body, the heat from them warming her, filling her and releasing the aching need she felt for him.

Below them, out in the garden room, the band made an announcement and the music stopped. The low chattering of conversation grew.

As if a switch had been flipped, her mind clicked back to the party and clarity seeped back in. She knew the band's schedule. If they were taking a break, it had to be ten twenty-five. A mass of confusion and desire flooded her, her emotions circling like a tornado low in her abdomen. No matter how much she wanted Reid, it wouldn't be fair—to either of them. She was leaving. "I-It's the grand opening," she said with a stammer, curling her back, breaking the connection between them. "I have to go."

His voice dropped into a low growl. "You can't dance like that for me, can't do *this*," he said with a wave of one hand, "and then leave me, darlin'."

But she didn't have a choice. "I have to," she whispered, straightening her dress. She looked at him, brushing the side of his face with the backs of her fingers. "I have to take care of something."

She hurried back to the party for a last farewell.

CHAPTER 17

REID LEANED against the wall in the stairwell, completely drained. The taste of Storie lingered on his tongue, the scent of her like a cloud of perfume floating around him, commingling with the aroma of the flowers she'd dried and had put everywhere. His frustration mounted, morphing into blistering anger. What—or who—was so important that she'd leave just when they were figuring things out? They needed to finish what they'd started, but there was more. He couldn't imagine being in Whiskey Creek without her. Hell, he couldn't imagine being in Austin—or anywhere—without Storie.

His mother had left him and Jiggs because she was too big for a little square town, but Reid suddenly realized that it didn't matter where he lived, as long as Storie was by his side.

Somewhere in the distance, an engine revved, gears grinding as it kicked into gear. Driving off a cliff—that was the right idea.

He wanted her like he'd never wanted anyone else. She

filled his mind with images of Sunday brunch and walks around the square. Long, leisurely afternoons in bed.

Love.

In Whiskey Creek.

Jesus, had he lost his mind? His happiness was *not* in a little square town, isn't that what his mother had told him? And now he was thinking of chucking all his plans, for what? For a woman who had secrets to spare and left him frustrated and cold?

He needed air. He needed to get her the hell out of his mind or he'd go crazy. He dug his keys from his pocket and left the stairs. *Guess Storie doesn't have to worry about not fitting in*, he thought wryly. The people had come out to see the new bookshop and its eclectic owners. The place would be a huge success.

He didn't see her as he plowed through the people, thank God. If he had, he might have gone caveman and dragged her upstairs. And it wouldn't have been against her will, either. He'd felt her body react to his touch. He knew she wanted him, but there was something else she wanted more. Something she'd left him to do.

And he had no idea what it was.

The band had wrapped up and the people were trickling out. He started to leave, changing his mind at the last second. Her apartment. She'd said she'd find someone else to work on it, but he'd be damned if he let her live in that disarray for another second. He turned and headed back into the shadows of the stairwell.

He took the stairs two at a time, ready to blaze through any repairs he could right this very minute. Practical? No. Necessary for his peace of mind? Yes.

He burst through the door, stopping in his tracks, staring at the space. "What the…?"

He'd been expecting the same disarray he'd seen a few

days ago, but was greeted by an immaculate room. The boxes were stacked against the back wall. The floors had been refinished.

"Impossible." Everything would have had to have been removed, the floors sanded, coats of stain and finish brushed on, and then it would have needed time to dry. He tested the floor. Not even tacky to the touch. "There's no freaking way." She couldn't have done this herself, so how?

He processed the rest of what he was seeing. The counters had been redone. New fixtures in the kitchenette. A new sink, too.

What the hell was going on? Something stirred in him and his mind circled around all the inconsistencies he'd noticed. Storie flicking her wrist and suddenly bubbles appeared in the bathtub. Another movement and the broken door slammed shut. The pressure of an invisible hand on his chest.

And now this. His head pounded. He cupped one hand behind his neck, pacing the room. What the hell *was* she?

He stood in front of the wall of boxes. They were stacked nearly to the ceiling. "How'd you do this, Storie?"

He processed the rest of the room, his gaze finally landing on an envelope in the center of the bed. His gut clenched when he saw Storie's straight up and down handwriting and Harper's name penned on the front.

He knew he should take it to Harper, but he ripped it open instead, unfolding the single sheet of stationery. Reading it sent a knife thrashing through his insides, the sentences burning into his mind.

One sentence shot out in front of all the others.

I'm a witch.

His mind whirled over what that meant. Was she a freaking Wiccan? One of those goddess mothers?

A freaking witch, whatever that meant, right next door to him.

He kept reading. His gut clenched when he realized what she was saying. She was leaving for good, meeting her mother at the lake. She'd told him it wouldn't matter after tonight. Now he understood.

I'm sorry to break our pact, she wrote, *but she needs me. My brother and sister need me.*

"No, *I* need you," he ground out. He let loose a string of curses, raked his hand through his hair, and crumpled the note in his fist. He wanted to ignore the part about her being a witch, but as he tried to push the idea out of his mind, he remembered her standing on the tailgate of her daddy's truck, arms stretched upward. What if she hadn't been basking in the rain? He tried to accept what he was thinking. Holy shit, what if she'd actually been *summoning* the thunder and lightning?

The last line of the message throbbed in his mind. *I have a family there*, she'd written. *It's where I belong.*

"No, it's not," he said. He wanted to throttle her for not seeing what was so obviously in front of her. "Harper *is* your family. *This* is where you belong."

Right here in Whiskey Creek, with him.

Family. He'd been running, too, always thinking he belonged somewhere else, that a little square town wasn't big enough to hold him. But with Storie, the town felt bigger. His life felt bigger. He had Jiggs and The Speakeasy. He had everything he wanted, but no matter where he went, if Storie wasn't there, it wouldn't matter.

Christ. He prayed he wasn't too late. He shoved the note in his pocket and raced back downstairs, plowing through the stragglers in the front room, hurrying to his truck parked in front of the bar, and heading for the lake.

CHAPTER 18

STORIE TORE around the corner in her Jeep. A tear rolled down her cheek. She hadn't been able to find Harper to say good-bye. What would she have said, anyway? *I'm leaving my dream to go to some otherworld with my mother, who, by the way, is a witch, and I'll live happily ever after with my brother and sister who I've never met.*

She swiped at another tear. Yeah, that would go over real well. She'd left the letter, but couldn't imagine Harper reading it. Would she understand? *Could* she?

She'd miss Scarlett and Piper. That was the thing that killed her most of all. She loved those girls like they were her own flesh and blood. She hadn't had a family, so she'd made her own with Harper and her daughters. Suddenly the idea of reuniting with a family she'd never known felt like an anvil around her neck, dragging her down.

And Reid...

"No." She pushed him out of her mind. She couldn't think about how he'd invaded every cell of her body since the day she'd learned the truth about her mother, or how seeing him again had charged every one of those cells with electricity.

She pounded the steering wheel with her hands, stifling the scream in her throat.

"It doesn't matter." He was leaving Whiskey Creek, anyway. One foot out of town, he'd said.

He'd only tried to seduce her to get into her building, not her pants. He'd manipulated her from the start, convincing Buddy Garland to beg off the job, sauntering in like a damn prince, ready to save the day. If she kept those facts front and center she could forget the rest.

So what if he rocked the rugged cowboy look like nobody's business? So what if running her hands through his hair sent shivers dancing over her skin? So what if that half-cocked smile he flashed beckoned her, even when she was alone in her bed just imagining him?

She drove over the bumpy dirt road, rumbling toward the old fishing shack just up from the shoreline. A sound in the backseat of the Jeep jolted her back to the present. She whipped her head around.

"Shelton!" The little mutt terrier sat squarely on the seat. She slammed on the brakes, swerving off the dirt road. "What are you doing here?"

The dog growled, but didn't budge.

Storie stared at her. She couldn't say why, but she had a feeling deep in her gut that she could understand her.

"You're on your own, Shelton." She was just a dog, and not even *her* dog.

She pulled back onto the road. Shelton barked, pawing at the driver's seat, but Storie ignored the dog. The fishing cabin came into view. The same spot at the lake where she'd come when she was twenty years old. The same place she'd first summoned thunder and lightning, to feel her power coursing through her. The same place she'd first seen Reid.

Shelton barked again.

"Funny how it all comes full circle, isn't it, Shelton?" she said.

Storie checked the rearview mirror as she drew closer to the meeting place, gasping, wrenching the steering wheel. Shelton wasn't sitting in the backseat. Instead, a young bohemian-looking woman with layered, shaggy hair the color of ochre, bracelets jangling on her wrists, and wide gold-flecked eyes held on to the front seats as the Jeep swerved off the road and plowed into the underbrush. Storie slammed on the brakes, threw the Jeep into park, and jumped out.

"Chill," the woman said, exiting the car, too.

"Chill?" Storie gaped. "Chill? Who the hell *are* you?"

"No need to repeat yourself."

"Who are you?" She recognized her from the café earlier, but she'd never seen her around town. Still, she was familiar. Could be the nose, she realized, straight and perfectly shaped with the slightest curve on either side.

Just like her own.

"My name's Astrid," the woman said, her voice sharp. "Your sister."

Storie was speechless, but the woman kept talking. "First things first." She cocked her arm at the elbow and aimed a thin, pointed stick at her. It shone in the moonlight, black and decorated with colorful flowers.

She snapped her wrist, waving the wand in a Bibbidi-Bobbidi-Boo circle, and then stood back, folding her arms over her chest. "Well, I'm not your fairy godmother, but it'll do."

Storie looked down at herself. Her dress had been replaced by jeans and a white ribbed tank top. Her thong and boots remained, and her sister hadn't conjured up a bra, but she still felt more comfortable in what she considered her standard daily uniform. "Is this what people wear in your magical world? 'Cause it's pretty much what I wear all the time."

Astrid scoffed. "So I noticed."

She stared. "Right. Shelton, the dog."

Astrid laughed. "I debated. I actually considered a potbellied pig, but I figured a stray dog was more realistic."

Storie nodded, still hung up on the whole shape-shifter thing. "Can you turn yourself into whatever you want?"

"Used to be able to. Not so much now. Our powers are depleted, but I guess mommy dearest told you all about that, right? Is that how she convinced you to go back with her?"

Storie nodded slowly. The cloud cover that had been hovering in the night sky moved and suddenly the full moon shone down on them. A full moon. Her mother had mentioned it, but now she shivered, a fleeting thought of how cliché it was that the moon was full on the very night she was crossing over.

Astrid nodded, tucking the front layers of her hair behind her ears. She had a carefree look to her, more gypsy than witch, but Storie would lay down money that men stopped in their tracks just to look at her. Like Helen of Troy. "Yes," she said.

"Yes, what?"

"We can only get through when the moon is full. That's why she has to take you tonight."

"You can read minds, too?"

"If the intentions are clear. Plus we're connected, you and I. And Declan. Triplets."

Connected. Woven together. Storie's head felt thick and heavy. She tried to wrap her mind around everything that was happening. Finally, she asked, "Get through what?" She peered into the darkness. "Where? How does it work?"

"God, you really are green, aren't you?" Astrid said with a short laugh. "It's a portal." She glided back to the Jeep, leaning against the red metal. "It's where you came through the first time. When our father escaped with you."

She stared, a chill winding through her. So that's why she felt a connection to this place.

"I've never had any witchy training," Storie said, defending her lack of abilities. She paced, her mind racing. This was too much to take in. Leaving her home, even if it had only been her home for a short while, and going to someplace foreign and magical... It wasn't what she wanted.

"You can't go back," Astrid said, her lips tightening.

She stopped at the front headlights, whipping around. "I'm here, aren't I?"

Astrid strode to her, putting both hands on her shoulders. The wand was gone, she noticed. A nifty trick. She didn't even *have* a wand. Her sister was right. She really was green.

"I mean," Astrid said, lowering her voice to a dark whisper, "you can't go with Millicent to the other side."

A wave of fear slithered over her. "Why?"

"It's a long story. Suffice it to say, the council has sanctioned her. The other side is a dark place, and our mother is more dark than light. She started to turn after our father took you away. She's been trying to get to you ever since, but they'd made a pact. You were protected."

Storie sank down on the running board of the Jeep. So Millicent only wanted to use her?

"The council's issued infractions against her," Astrid continued. "But the pact died with our father, and now, if she brings you back, the three of us will be together again and she can tap into our collective magic. She'll regain the power the council took from her and we'll be left with nothing."

She stared at Astrid, her mind racing. "And that wouldn't be good?"

"No. That wouldn't be good. She's gone dark, and when she taps into our power, she'll kill us."

Kill them? That certainly wasn't the mother she'd longed for all these years. "So what do we do?"

"Fight her," Astrid said, "but it won't be easy without Declan."

"Where is he?"

"He's on the council of elders. He helped me sneak out to find you, but he can't go. Not yet. Leaving would be too dangerous for him. His powers are stronger than mine. My powers are weakening, and yours—" She laughed harshly. "Yours are practically nonexistent."

Storie stifled her indignation. It wasn't her fault her powers were feeble. "Not quite," she said, rotating her wrist and flicking it, pointing at the underbrush. The shrub rustled and a snake slithered out, followed by an armor-backed armadillo and a flurry of other creatures.

"I don't think you'll be able to defeat Millicent by making the critters scurry," Astrid said, shaking her head.

Before she could answer, the air turned thick and humid around them, so heavy and dense that she could see it shimmering.

"You're right, Astrid," a woman said from behind them. "Parlor tricks won't work."

Storie's heart shot to her throat. She recognized the voice. Her mother.

CHAPTER 19

REID SKIDDED to a stop at the circle of trees. Storie had told him that the lake was her sanctuary. He didn't know where she'd gone, but this was the only place that made sense. It's where she'd said she'd come fishing with her father. It seemed to be her safe place.

Dark clouds rolled in overhead, the humidity thick and stifling. Lightning illuminated the sky in a rapid one-two flash, the raucous crack of thunder reverberating moments later.

Storie.

He peered up, studying the sky, hoping for some clue so he could track her down. The air crackled with electricity. The epicenter was down the shoreline a hundred yards or so, where his truck wouldn't drive. He jumped out, realization dawning. She wasn't going to simply drive away with her mother. She was a witch, and that meant spells and portals and magical passageways.

"Storie!" he yelled as he ran. But the rolling thunder and the lapping of the water against the sand drowned out his voice. He stopped, getting his bearings, listening. The world seemed to swirl out of control around him, the sky crackling and alive, a network of squiggly glowing lines all around.

Witch. Storie's letter. Not a Wiccan or some powerless Earth goddess mother. A real witch. Holy fucking Christ.

From the corner of his eye, he caught a movement. Something white. He took off running at full speed, adrenaline pulsing through him.

He dodged the brush and vaulted over a log, pulling up short when he saw her. Déjà vu hit him, only this time fear spread like tendrils to every part of his body. She stood on a flat-topped rock, her arms stretched toward the sky, silver light glowing at the tips of her fingertips.

The bohemian woman Jason had been enraptured with stood motionless like a stone statue. He remembered talking to Storie in the tearoom, struggling with that damn shelf, and her mother showing up. Another witch. She'd done something to him and he'd lost minutes, frozen in time.

Shit. This wasn't good.

He didn't have any recourse against magic, but he wouldn't stand aside and do nothing. At the very least, he'd create a diversion. Hell, he'd die trying to help Storie, no matter what it took. He skirted around the pine trees, ducking out of sight and prowling quietly until he was hidden behind Storie's red Jeep.

* * *

Panic stole through Storie. Astrid had warned her, but Millicent had anticipated the betrayal and had immobilized her with some sort of spell. The same thing that she'd done to Reid that day in the tearoom.

Her *mother*. The word twisted in her mind. She'd been so stupid, choosing to leave The Storiebook Café, Harper and the girls, and Reid for a mother who wanted nothing more than to steal her powers and leave her for dead.

Her eyes burned as she tried to move her arms. She'd managed to reach up to the sky, concentrating every bit of her power to her fingers until the tips glowed with fire. Sweeping her arms to the left, over and over, the cloud cover rolled in, a thunderous roar undulating through the sky. Lightning speared through the darkness, but dizziness followed, her body turning limp and weak. Her legs buckled under her, but she gathered her strength and righted herself. She wouldn't let her mother ruin everything she'd worked so hard for. Not now. Not ever.

Astrid's frozen eyes were pinched and intent, as if she'd looked head-on into Medusa's eyes ready to do battle, but had lost.

The blinding light from above subsided, the turbulent clouds in motion above her, a heavy, warm rain falling in a torrent.

Millicent laughed, a high-pitched cackling sound that was brittle and sent a gust of shivers over Storie's skin. "Working the weather is rudimentary, daughter," she said, advancing slowly, as if she didn't have a care in the world. "Is that the best you can do?"

"I'm not going with you." Thanks to Astrid, Storie knew the truth. Without her, the sibling triad was incomplete, and her mother couldn't suck or steal or absorb their power. She didn't know how it worked, but there was no way in hell she was crossing over to the magical world.

"Astrid and Declan need you, Storie. You'll let them wither away and die? You'll let yourself go?"

"You sent me away," she said, the rain drenching her, the words of that short sentence unleashing all the anger and frustration and loneliness she'd felt since she was a child.

Her mother stared at her, oblivious to the roiling sky

above and the rain pelting them.

"He took you."

She shook her head, seeing in her mind how it must have played out. Her father's view had been jaded by Millicent, but… "He loved you. My father loved you," she said, her voice barely audible over the storm.

Millie laughed, the sound like a hyena cackling. "His mistake."

"You didn't love him back." That was clear, but she needed to hear it. To understand.

"I thought it was him," she said. "My powers were diminishing, and I was sure it was because he was an ordinary human."

"But it wasn't," she said, almost to herself. Her father's belief that witches and mortals couldn't be together had come from Millicent, but it wasn't true.

"I gave you to him and sent him away." She nodded and looked like she'd do it again if need be. "I thought getting rid of the mortal would be enough, but you're half mortal. Your brother and sister have his blood," she said, accusation lacing her voice. As if they'd all made a choice to be born to her and their mortal father.

"A mother's responsibility is to care for her children, not to destroy them."

Millicent glared at Astrid, frozen under a veil of gauze. "The three of you drained my power and your brother has grown strong, but even he is suffering. The time has come. The pact is broken. Now it's time to reclaim what is mine."

Storie backed up, casting another frantic look at Astrid. Still immobile, but—

She blinked, forcing another flash of lightning so she could see. Had Astrid blinked, or was the rippling light playing tricks with her vision? If she agreed to go with her mother, would it help Astrid, or would it simply be the end for all three of them, including Declan, the powerful brother she'd never met?

Millicent advanced, her pale face calm and soft. "My dear," she cooed, "your affairs are in order. Harper will thrive with the café. I'll see to it. If you come with me, her girls will find their happy endings. And you can be back where you belong, reunited with your family."

Her breath caught. Behind Millicent, Astrid pressed her arms down slowly, as if she were encased in a tube of viscous air, heavy and obtrusive. Storie had to stall, to figure out how to help Astrid escape. "And if I don't?"

"I'm not evil, daughter. You've no idea how I've missed you," her mother said, but that hard edge crept back into her voice. "I need to reunite my three children."

Yeah, right. Millicent needed them together to reclaim her failing power, that was the truth. She stepped back, shaking her head. "Astrid told me everything." She grabbed hold of the Jeep and scurried up, balancing on the full-sized spare tire mounted to the back tailgate. The platform wasn't as stable as being in the back of her daddy's truck, but it would do. "You haven't missed me," she retorted. "You need me. There's a big difference."

"That's true, but you're a witch and you belong in the magical world, not withering away in a ridiculous small town." Millicent's lips thinned. "Yes, I need you. Who do you need and who needs you?"

An image flashed in her mind, and she knew the answer—at least to the first question. Reid. She needed him. She *wanted* him, mortal or not. The question in her mind was, would he want her after he learned the truth?

A faint sound rose above the tumultuous sky. She glanced to the left and found her answer.

Reid! He crouched out of Millicent's sight, but he had to have heard everything.

The answer to her mother's questions flew out of her mouth before she could think. "I need Reid," she said, "and..."

She cast another quick look his way. He nodded, and she understood. He'd come for her. To fight for her. He knew who she was...*what* she was, and he'd come anyway. "And he needs me."

Millicent threw her head back and let loose a dark laugh. "It's a lovely dream, daughter, but love with a mortal man is fraught with peril. He can't understand you—not really—and in the end, you'll have to choose to live in his mortal world and forsake who you are, or you can come with me and be what you were born to be."

Storie dragged in a deep breath, her mind clearing, her panic subsiding. Power surged through her. There was an undeniable electrical charge between her and Reid that she'd never felt with anyone, and knew she never would again. And he was here. He'd come to stop her from leaving. She had to get through this so she could tell him how she felt. More than anything, she couldn't let him go. "It's an easy choice," she said. "I choose him."

But Millicent shook her head. "It's the witching hour, my dear, and I'm afraid the choice is no longer yours to make." She lifted her arms, a blood-red wand appearing in one hand.

Storie acted without thinking. Her arms flew up, pointing to the sky, and she uttered the spell she'd crafted when she'd been twenty years old and had first truly harnessed her control over the sky. She hadn't used her magic, and prayed that using it now didn't completely wipe her out and that she could summon what she needed to fight her mother. The dark clouds gathered, swirling and spiraling, as gray fingers feathered together, like a hand reaching toward them.

The moving sky was enough to break Millicent's concentration. She faltered, and at the same moment Reid shot out from behind the Jeep, sprinting toward Astrid. He ran straight for her, as if he knew that she was stuck inside an enchantment and sheer physical force was his only chance of freeing her. He accepted what was happening, and in that moment, Storie knew she'd made the right choice.

She cast her eyes back to her mother. Millicent had seen Reid and murmured something, but Storie jerked her arm and one finger of the clouds grew instantly, spiraling, gathering strength. She spun her own finger, moving the funnel, guiding it like a puppet master until it touched down between Millicent and Astrid, forcing her mother back.

The vigor of the tornado knocked Millicent off her feet. She landed in a heap, struggling to untwine her caftan from under her jumbled legs.

The spell trapping Astrid broke, the air bubble that encased her rupturing with the force of Reid barreling into it. The threads broke into wispy pieces, floating up like a spider web that had been torn apart. Reid's arm shot toward it, grabbing for the gauzy strands.

"Get your mother out of here!" he yelled, pushing Astrid toward them.

Astrid rushed to Storie, gripping her by the arm and turning to face their mother. "She's not going," her sister said, her shiny black flower-covered wand appearing in her hand. Storie's body tingled, her skin rippling from the contact with Astrid. Energy flashed across her. She grew stronger, and her magic swelled inside her. Siblings reunited. Their powers were joining, she realized. Commingling and gaining strength. She didn't have a wand, but maybe she didn't need one.

From the corner of her eye, she saw Reid circle around the truck, appearing again behind Millicent, and she took her cue.

She held tight to Astrid, flinging her arm out, fingers pointed at Millicent. A spear of light shot out from the tip of her index finger. A wave of dizziness crashed over her and the coil of glowing red faltered, crackling like lightning. But she drew in a breath, planted her boots firmly in the sand, and held her arm steady. The storm gathered strength again, encircling Millicent like a lasso. At the same moment, Reid rushed toward Millicent, throwing the filmy strands of webbing over her. Millicent snatched at them, trying to pull them off, but they settled on her and cascaded over her head, draped her shoulders, and stunned her into submission.

Storie edged toward her, her arm outstretched, but shaky. She stopped in front of her mother, grabbing hold of the transparent strands of film covering her. She wound her arm in a circle, wrapping her up tighter and tighter until Millicent was immobile.

"You're making the wrong choice," her mother managed to say, her voice faint and strained under the veil. "It's not over."

"I'm not going back," she said.

Millicent looked from Storie to Reid and back, her eyes wide with disbelief. Storie wound the threads tighter and tighter, fighting her weakening limbs and directing all her focus on immobilizing her mother. Her arm trembled. She wasn't sure how much longer she could hold her magic steady, but after another minute, Millicent finally let out a shrill cry and slumped to the ground.

As Reid sprinted to her, she let out the breath she hadn't known she'd been holding. "Is she…will she…"

Astrid took her hand, their strength melding together again until Storie felt stable. "She'll be fine," Astrid said. "Without Declan's powers, the spell won't hold her for long."

Storie's mind scrambled to make sense of what had happened. Her sister's power had blended with hers, allowing her to defeat Millicent—at least for now.

"She won't give up?"

Astrid laughed, but the humor didn't reach her eyes. "You won a small battle, Storie, but the war is still raging."

Storie released her hold on the storm. The rain stopped, the full moon vibrant in the velvety blackness of the sky, the entire shoreline of the lake illuminated as if it were daylight.

"So you're staying here," Reid said to her.

Storie nodded, for once, completely sure that she'd made the right decision. No doubt. No reservations. Just confidence that her happily ever after was right here in Whiskey Creek. "I'm staying."

"What about her?" Reid notched his head toward Millicent.

"She's right. It is the witching hour," Astrid said. "I have to take her back while I still can. Declan and the council will punish her, and she'll be kept at bay, at least for a while, but she's right about our powers." Astrid looked off into the distance, brushing her loose curls back from her face, her bangle bracelets tinkling on her wrist. "They're fading. Eventually, if the three of us are not reunited, we will wither away."

"Just like she said."

Astrid nodded. "She won't give up."

"Will you be safe?" Storie asked. She'd just found her sister; she certainly didn't want to lose her again.

Instead of answering, Astrid gave her a quick hug. "I'll be back and we'll figure out what to do."

"Will Declan come with you?"

She shrugged. "He can't, at least not while he's on the council of elders. But at some point, yes, he'll have to if we're to unite our power."

Storie stood by Reid, tears burning behind her eyelids as Astrid glided toward their mother and crouched next to her. She muttered something inaudible, the air rippled, and they were gone.

CHAPTER 20

Storie cast a nervous glance at Reid, who was inspecting the spot Millicent and Astrid had been moments before. The moonlight broke through the cloud cover, the lake shimmering from the sliver of light. He knew she was a witch, and he hadn't run for the hills. Thick, soft, dark hair dusted the neckline of his soaked shirt. Smile lines etched either side of his eyes. That little tuft of hair under his lower lip sent her stomach into a frenzy.

But did he really need her?

His tattoo peeked out from under his sleeve. A charge shot through her body as she watched him. She wanted him, wanted to be connected with him. Never wanted to lose him.

"You okay, darlin'?"

She blinked, her vision coming into focus. He stood in front of her, his eyes dark and smoldering in the bright moonlight. "I've spent years imaging how it would feel to meet my mother." She forced a laugh. "Let me tell you, my dreams were nothing like this."

"Your father tried to protect you with a pact."

She nodded. "He didn't even know about my brother and sister. She wasn't much of a mother."

They stood together in weighty silence. After a minute Storie broke it. "You kept your dad's secret. You'd do anything for him."

He nodded. "I would."

"And I just sent my mother away."

"You did what you had to. She's a...a witch."

Storie held her breath before asking the next question. "Do you believe that?"

His gaze met hers. "I witnessed it, Storiebook."

"And...?" She'd felt like an outsider her entire life, never fitting in, always on the run with her father. *Mortals and witches don't mix*. But that wasn't the whole truth. Her father and mother hadn't worked out, but that didn't mean she and Reid couldn't find common ground. If he accepted her...

"And I like the spell you have me under," he said with a wink.

She drew up, half laughing, half indignant. "I don't have you under a spell!"

His lips drew into a line, and the intensity of his gaze seared through her until her blood boiled and her core ached. Her smile faded. She might as well have been naked to him. The rain had soaked her T-shirt and it clung to her body like a second skin, and she had a feeling of déjà vu. They'd been in this very place the night before she'd left Whiskey Creek the first time.

He'd witnessed her magic then, and she'd taunted him with her body. She'd been in control then, barely, but now her mind raced, her pulse throbbed, and heat swelled in her. It coursed through her body until she was a swirling mass of fluttering desire.

He closed the gap between them. "You're a witch," he said, as if he could read the worry on her mind.

Her heart slid to her throat. If he still wanted her, she wouldn't walk away this time. "Does that scare you?"

"Nothing about you could scare me, Storiebook."

She smiled, her voice soft. "It scares me, especially now."

"It's what's always made you feel different?"

She nodded as she slid her hand under his shirt, spreading her palm against his muscled abdomen. She let it rest there for a few seconds before sliding it down. The thin line of hair leading to the waistband of his jeans tickled her fingers. She swallowed, holding her breath. She'd been waiting for him to chastise her for lying to him about her magic, expecting him to turn and walk away like she'd turned and walked away from him, but he didn't do either.

No, he dragged his smoldering gaze back up and looked into the depths of her eyes, a wolfish expression on his face that sent a shiver up her spine and a tingling sensation dancing over her body.

The corner of his mouth tilted up wickedly and he dipped his head, bringing his lips to hers. "Looks like we're back where we started."

* * *

A witch. Reid shook his head, that aspect of who she was settling into his reality.

"Storie Rae." He pulled her closer, savoring the feel of their bodies pressed together. "I love you, you know," he said, the moonlight casting a soft light over her.

A shudder wound through her. "But the magic…" she said, trailing off as if she were afraid of the barrier that might create between them.

As if he'd forgotten.

"With magic. Without magic. None of it matters. It's you I love, not your powers."

"But my mother…she'll be back."

"Tell me what happened," he said, drawing her closer.

She paused, looking afraid she'd spook him.

"Don't be afraid, darlin'. I'm here to stay."

Storie sucked in a deep breath, nodded as if she finally believed him. "She told me she and my father made a pact that she would stay away. After he passed, the pact was broken."

A pact to stay away from your own daughter. That was neck-and-neck with walking out and simply not ever coming back. "So you never knew her at all?"

Storie shook her head. "She gave my father seeds to her favorite flower. They're delicate and sweet and remind me of cinnamon and nutmeg and…something else I can't really describe, but—" She backed away. "Oh! The astrids! Your dad! That's what my dad gave him. The oil from the flowers. It's like…"

"Magic?" He laughed. Even after everything she'd been through tonight, and over the last few days, months…years… she was thinking about what he needed. What Jiggs needed.

"We'll worry about that tomorrow. Jiggs'll make his deal with the spirits company and let me tell you, he'll be a bitch to live with. And I'll have to put up with him." He shook his head, still not quite believing that everything had worked out so perfectly. "A moonshine millionaire. I never saw *that* coming."

"I've been growing those flowers since I was a kid," Storie said. "I never knew they had power."

"I bet there's a lot you don't know, darlin'."

"Astrid said she'll come back. To teach me, I hope."

"You just keep practicing what you know. It'll all work out fine." His adrenaline from the fight with Storie's mother was crashing and it was all he could do to think straight.

Desire like he'd never known filled him completely. He was done talking. For now, he watched in fascination as she stepped away from him, turned to the Jeep, pointed, and notched her wrist.

She faltered, as if she had a sudden lapse of energy, but then she moved again and a quilt from the backseat floated through the air like a flying carpet, settling on the wet, sandy shore in front of them.

When he turned back to her, her white ribbed tank was knotted under her breasts, her belly button ring glimmering as it caught the moonlight, beckoning his touch.

Another déjà vu moment hit, sending him back to the first time he'd seen her looking like this. How one woman could elicit such a range of emotions, from lust to friendship to stability to a future, was a mystery, but they all surged through him, intertwining into a mass of love.

He made a sound deep in his throat. "I kinda like this magical thing," he said, closing the distance between them.

She stood in front of him, her soaked tank top clinging to her perfect breasts, her nipples hard buttons straining against the sheer, wet cotton. She probably could have used some spell to dry the fabric, but she hadn't. It was evident that she had a thing about tormenting him, and truth be told, he didn't mind this particular kind of torture.

Her chest rose and fell as her breath grew ragged under his searing gaze. In one quick movement, he reached behind his neck, grabbed hold of his shirt, and yanked it off, dropping it to the ground.

Her fingers danced over the intricate design of the tattoo on his right arm, the magic of her touch instantly making him grow hard. As if she sensed the reaction, her hand fluttered to the button of his jeans, but he stopped her, cupping her hand with his.

"I'm not going anywhere, Storie Rae," he said, the words heavy as they left his lips. "But are you sure?"

She lifted her chin, rising on her toes until her lips brushed his. "I'm sure." And then her mouth was on his, eliciting a sound from deep inside him. He groaned, pulling her nearer, closing the space between them.

So she was sure.

They were going to do this on his terms. "No magic," he said, his voice low as he spoke against her lips.

"No magic," she said with a moan, dragging her hands through his hair and pulling him back to her.

"This time, anyway," he amended. Maybe later, after they'd explored each other, knew each other inside and out, maybe then she could use magic. And he knew there would be a later.

He kissed her again, a shudder passing over her body. He grabbed her hips, walking backward, bringing her with him. backing her up against the Jeep, clasping her head in his hands, scraping his fingers through her hair as he found her mouth again. Tilting her head back to expose her neck, he trailed his lips along her jaw, down to the top edge of her shirt.

She didn't have to try. She was magic in every way. He grabbed her by the waist and lifted her, setting her on on the tailgate. Then he looked at her. God, she was perfect.

Slowly, he felt the button of his pants come loose. The next instant, they'd vanished all together.

"You're being a bad witch," he said, stepping away.

But she shook her head, used his shoulders to brace herself as she jumped down from the Jeep, and undid the fastenings on her jeans. "No, I'm being a good witch," she said, flashing him the most devilish smile he'd ever seen.

In seconds, she'd stripped out of her soaked jeans and

boots, standing before him in just a triangle of lace. His head filled with raw desire, his pulse thundering in his head.

"You're a very good bad witch," he murmured as he took her from the tailgate to the quilt.

Storie. She was all he could ever want.

CHAPTER 21

STORIE DRAGGED in a bolstering breath as she draped her leg over Reid's thigh, rolling him onto his back until she straddled him.

"Beautiful," he murmured, his gaze sweeping over her.

"I need you to—"

He snaked a hand around to the back of her neck, pulling her down and kissing her again. "To what?" he asked, his lips scarcely leaving hers long enough to utter the question.

"I need to know if you're leaving," she said, biting her lip, deathly afraid of his response. What if he hadn't changed his mind about leaving Whiskey Creek? Could she be with him now, knowing that he wouldn't be around for the long term?

He kissed her neck, trailing his lips over her collarbone and across her chest.

She tried to restrain the moan climbing up her throat, but he used his tongue inventively and the sound escaped from her throat, unbidden.

"I'm never leaving you," he murmured.

Those four words wound through her, surrounding her heart, throttling her full-speed into the passion she'd been trying to keep at bay. This…this was what she wanted. Her connection with Reid filled the emptiness she'd had inside her forever. She slid her hands over him, her fingers exploring the hard lines of his stomach, tangling through the dusting of hair on his chest. He was perfect.

The cool air of the night rushed over them, goose bumps rising on her skin, but the heat from his touch, from their bodies moving together, warmed her from the inside out.

Her heart thudded in her ears. These were Reid's hands on her hips. His searing gaze scorching her skin as he took in every bit of her.

"Storie Rae," he murmured. Her name rolled off his tongue as if he'd been saying it all his life. She flattened her hands on his chest. He'd said no magic, but she used her powers to slide out the pins holding her hair. Her curls loosened, tumbling in a gentle motion, the ends tickling his cheek.

"Nifty trick," he said with a husky laugh.

She smiled down at him. "I'm full of nifty tricks," she said, "but I can never make you do anything you don't want to do."

"I want to do this." He pulled her down to him, bringing his lips to hers, his touch slow. Intentional. Intimate. "I want you, Storie. Since I first saw you, it's always been you."

She nodded, sure her eyes told him the same story, her truth. He'd haunted her dreams since the last time they'd been at the lake, and now here they were again, coming full circle and ready to start a new life together.

She looked into his eyes, sucked into the sea of blue-gray. His desires were laid out before her. They'd found each other, and there was no going back.

She rocked against him, their movements binding them together. Her breath grew ragged in her chest as she felt herself peak, then a moment of stillness before warmth radiated out from her core, encircling her heart, breaking into rolling waves of oblivion.

He let go the next moment, a low, guttural moan slipping from his lips as he came undone, their unfinished business complete, but opening the door for a new chapter.

***

Reid held Storie close, her head tucked into the hollow between his shoulder and neck. They lay comfortable in each other's arms for what felt like mere minutes, but was probably closer to an hour. Too content to move and sever what they'd finally found with each other.

"Millicent the Malevolent," Storie said after a while.

Reid laughed. "What?"

"Every evil witch needs a moniker, right? Millicent the Malevolent. The name fits her."

"I guess it does."

"She's not going to give up until she reunites the three of us so she can steal our powers, you know."

He knew she was trying to give him an out. He didn't bite. She was stuck with him, through boring days, moonshine, and magic battles. "Like I said, just keep practicing what you know."

She sighed, arching her neck and stretching until her lips brushed against his. At the same time she waved her hand, sweeping the dark clouds that still hovered above them clear away. Twinkling lights were left in their wake, dancing and flickering like beacons. "I think I've loved you since you tried to rescue me from drowning," she said with a smile, nipping at his lower lip.

The light sparkling from above reflected off the water. Her touch sent an electric charge through him. He was ready for more Storie. He'd never felt so at peace. Not some spell, he hoped. He wanted his feelings to be all his own, no powers or conjuring involved.

He laughed. "I think I have, too."

Her fingers traced the tattoo around his biceps, heating the lines as if it were suddenly on fire. "When did you get this?" she asked, her voice soft and sleepy.

"The summer you left Whiskey Creek," he said.

"What's it mean?" She moved the pads of her fingers along the intricate pattern and weave.

"It's a Celtic tribal symbol." He knew the pattern inside and out. His mother had left a necklace behind with the three-cornered knots. One represented the body, one the mind, and the last the spirit, and when linked together, created a circle. Two circles overlapping represented two people who've found each other.

He'd gotten the tattoo as a touchstone for the love his parents had once had, for the love he'd wanted to have but found so elusive. It was a constant reminder to him of what could be, but suddenly it was a symbol of what he had.

He pondered her question for a minute, trying to figure out how to put it into words. "It's about finding a happy ending," he finally said.

She smiled, and he knew she understood what he meant. He rolled her onto her back, bracing himself over her, looking into her eyes. The woman he loved. The woman he'd waited for. The witch next door, bringing magic into his life. "It means everlasting love," he said, and he kissed her.

The End

. . .

*T*hank you for reading *Storiebook Charm*. Readers often decide what to read based on reviews. I am very appreciative of all reviews and would be grateful if you'd take a few minutes to share your thoughts about this book HERE.

*K*eep going for to read a sample of Murder in Devil's Cove, and join my newsletter!

The truth is buried in the pages

MURDER IN DEVIL'S COVE

A BOOK MAGIC MYSTERY

"A magical blend of books, mystery, and smart sleuthing."
~NYT and USA bestselling author, Ellery Adams

MELISSA BOURBON

NATIONAL BESTSELLING AUTHOR

READ AN EXCERPT FROM MURDER IN DEVIL'S COVE

CASSANDRA LANE HAWTHORNE stood on the main fishing pier in Devil's Cove staring out at the harbor, grasping the pendant she wore around her neck. The breeze blew across the Sound, whipping her hair into her face. The same feeling of foreboding she'd had since the day she'd met her husband filled her. Her insides were a dry sponge slowly expanding with water. "You're not going to take him," she said. Her voice was carried away on the breath of wind. She spoke again, louder this time. "You won't take him!"

"Take who, Mama?" Cassie's six-year-old daughter, Pippin, tugged at the fabric of Cassie's dress.

"Nobody." She took Pippin's hand and squeezed. "It's cold. Come on, let's go home."

They walked along the wooden slats of the pier, Cassie's white canvas sneakers silent next to the slap slap slap of Pippin's sandals. The irony of her daughter's name wasn't lost on Cassie. Leo was a Tolkien fanatic. He and a group of friends had called themselves The Fellowship all through college. And when it came time to name their children, he'd longed for names from Tolkien's classics. Their son, born seconds before Pippin, they'd named Grey, after Gandalf the Grey. And their daughter had been named after Peregrin, one of Frodo Baggin's best hobbit friends. Pippin for short.

Cassie had never read the books, but she loved her husband.

She wanted no book to enter their home, but she'd made concessions for Leo. He kept his personal collection under lock and key in the office of the sea captain's house they'd bought in Devil's Cove when they'd first married. Cassie would have nothing to do with Leo's books, now more than ever. Her fear about what they could tell her about the future was much greater than her temptation.

Her skirt whipped around her legs, billowing out behind her. This weather…the ocean…the outer banks of North Carolina. She loved every bit of it. Everything except waiting for Leo to come home to her. Waiting for the sea to give her husband back to her.

They walked together, Pippin's feet moving in double-time to keep up with Cassie's longer stride. "Library!" Pippin yanked on Cassie's hand and pulled her toward the two story house that had years ago been converted. The word LIBRARY was spelled across the eaves over the small porch entry. A blue sign with a figure holding a book was secured in the ground at the sidewalk, denoting the building as the town's library.

It was a place Cassie never stepped foot into.

"Another day, lovee," she said to Pippin, pulling her along. She placed one hand on her pregnant belly. Through the fog, the town's bookstore came into view. That was another building she refused to go into.

All books had a history.

All books told stories—those written on the pages, and those between the lines.

Cassie wanted nothing to do with any of them.

The library and the bookstore were on opposite sides of the street. If Cassie took the conventional path, she'd have to pass one or the other. Instead, she marked a diagonal to cross the street, leaving the sidewalk before they got to the library, planning to step up onto the opposite sidewalk a few yards past the bookstore. It was the only way to miss them both.

She muttered under her breath. Only her Aunt Rose thought of their family magic as a blessing. But Cassie only saw it as a curse. Her sister Lacy and their mother had both died in childbirth. Her great-grandfather, grandfather, and father had all been taken by the sea. Cassie had left the west coast and the only family she had only to fall in love with Leonardo Jay Hawthorne, a bookish fisherman from the Outer Banks. Her destiny to live by the sea was fulfilled. She couldn't escape, that was the truth of the matter.

Cassie grabbed hold of Pippin's hand and hurried on, dipping her head against the cold wind. She touched her swollen belly again. She'd survived childbirth, but would she be able to tempt fate twice? And what about Leo. He'd joined the Lane's through marriage, but had Cassie only transferred the curse to him? Would he be able to escape the fate of the men in her family? For that matter, how could she keep Grey off the water and safe?

A elderly woman, her head lowered, emerged from the bookstore. A cobalt blue scarf covered her hair, its tail whipping behind her. She pulled her woolen coat tight around herself. Instead of staying on the sidewalk, the old woman stepped into the street. Just as Cassie was doing, she cut a diagonal. Cassie looked at the older woman as she and Pippin approached her, gasping when the woman suddenly looked up, her tiger eyes boring into her. A shiver slithered up Cassie's spine.

In an instant, the fog thickened, covering Devil's Cove

with a heavy blanket of mist. Something hit the ground as the old woman dropped her gaze again and passed them. Without thinking, Cassie bent to pick up the fallen object. The moment she did, her heart hammered in her chest. She looked at what she held.

It was a tattered copy of Homer's The Odyssey.

Cassie cried out. Dropped the book.

It landed on its spine. The pages fell open.

Before Cassie could stop her, Pippin scooped it up and held it out to her, holding it open. "She dropped it."

Cassie looked over her shoulder. "Wait," she called out, but the fog had swallowed the woman.

A chill swept through Cassie as she looked down at the open pages of the book her daughter held. Her eyes scanned the words and her heart climbed to her throat.

... *S*o all that has been duly done. Listen now, I will tell you

all, but the very god himself will make you remember.

You will come first of all to the Sirens, who are enchanters

of all mankind and whoever comes their way; and that man

who unsuspecting approaches them, and listens to the Sirens

singing, has no prospect of coming home and delighting

his wife and little children as they stand about him in greeting,

but the Sirens by the melody of their singing enchant him.

they sit in their meadow, but the beach before it is piled with the boneheads of men now rotted away, and the skins shrivel upon them.

"No. No, no, no." Cassie fell to her knees, unable to hold in her sobs.

Read More…

FIND MELISSA ONLINE

VISIT Melissa's website
http://melissabourbon.com

JOIN her online book club at https://www.facebook.com/groups/BookWarriors/

FOLLOW her on Facebook at facebook.com/AuthorMelissaBourbonWinnieArcher

FOLLOW her on Instagram @Bookishly_Cozy

ABOUT THE AUTHOR

Melissa Bourbon Ramirez is the national bestselling author of more than twenty-five mystery books, including the Magical Dressmaking Mystery series, the Book Magic Mysteries, and the Bread Shop Mysteries, written as Winnie Archer. She is a former middle school English teacher who gave up the classroom in order to live in her imagination full time. Melissa, a California native who has lived in Texas and Colorado, now calls the southeast home. Her dogs, Bean, the pug, and Dobby, the chug keep her company while she writes. Melissa lives in North Carolina with her educator husband, Carlos. She is beyond fortunate to be living the life of her dreams.

- facebook.com/MelissaBourbonWinnieArcherBooks
- instagram.com/bookishly_cozy
- bookbub.com/authors/melissa-bourbon
- pinterest.com/MbourbonWArcher
- amazon.com/Melissa-Bourbon/e/B0079QNXQQ

Made in the USA
Coppell, TX
21 July 2023

19448804R00125